Riffs

A Collection of Short Stories

Michael G. Casey

ISBN 978-1-8384789-0-2

First edition, 2021

Published by Azimuth Publishing
Dublin, Ireland

Layout, cover design / painting by iCulture

Please visit michaelgcasey.com

ABOUT THIS BOOK

THE SHORT STORIES in this volume are conceived as riffs—memorable patterns of music and conversation that will fall like blessings on the inner ear.

The stories embrace a wide range of human experience from memories of childhood to a first encounter with musical harmony (and dissonance).

But they are not all sweetness and light. They reach into dark corners of obsessive bureaucracy, gender confusion in the world of sports, tragedy and loss, brutal hierarchies, abuse of power in a nursing home and a TV station, sexual harassment and rape on campus.

A number of stories stretch into quirky areas such as Munchausen's Syndrome (with a twist), the usurpation of human contact by technology, and the strange effects of parallel universes.

A panoptic fly which features in one story, buzzes everywhere and sees all things in the human sphere.

"The cleverness in each story is in the way it turns. These are not all good people, but they are credible and they fight, sometimes most curiously, for what they want. They pivot their world to what they believe they need, sometimes with method, sometimes in chaos, sometimes disastrously. These are highly engaging stories

built around the lone or clashing perspectives of stubborn people in a recalcitrant world."
—Peter FitzGerald

BOOKS PREVIOUSLY PUBLISHED
BY MICHAEL G. CASEY

Come Home, Robbie, a novel, published by The
O'Brien Press, 1990

> "…page-turning urgency … spine-
> tingling compulsion … the sheer quality
> of the writing lends the story some of the
> stature of heroic tragedy."
> —The Education Times

Treadmill, an award-winning Chapbook of short
stories, published by Tipperary Arts Centre and
Start Magazine, 2008

> "…Casey brings to life vivid characters
> who captivate, amuse and engage …
> (He) has a wry observation and quick
> wit."
> —Mike McCormack

*Ireland's Malaise: The Troubled Personality of the
Irish Economy*, published by The Liffey Press,
2010

> "…(Casey) shows the same Confucian
> wisdom as his hero, T.K. Whitaker, in
> his brilliant new book."
> —Eoghan Harris, The Sunday

Independent

The Visit, a novel, published by The Anaphora Press, 2011

> "…a small Irish town deals with a major event … an interesting addition to the genre … clear-eyed … vivid description…"
> —Denis Fahey, Historian

> "…a lovely clear prose style … some great characters and beautifully crafted vignettes."
> —Stella Kane, Quartet Books Ltd

Broken Circle, a collection of poetry, due to be published by Salmon Press in Spring 2019

> "…very powerful, intelligent poems made their presence known immediately … (Casey) uses casuistry and persuasiveness to rival Robert Browning's dramatic Monologues…"
> —Derek Selen

Michael G. Casey's most recent novels, *Smudged Mascara*, *Maura's Dance with Uncle Sam*, *The Killing of Ros Grenham*, *Proving Ground* and *Neap Tide*, from Azimuth Publishing, are available in Kindle and print versions through Amazon. So too are the selection of short stories, *Divers Kinds*, and two collections of plays, *Joyce's Wake and Other Full-length Plays* and *Joyce at Last and Other Short Plays*.

CONTENTS

DEDICATION

For Gráinne

LAYING DORMANT

BREATHING HEAVILY, ANTHONY helped her into his hotel room where she fell in a sprawl on the bed; a shaft of moonlight picked out the helpless, drugged smile on her face. She had good teeth; he couldn't deny that. She twisted and turned for a while, then, with a long sigh, fell into a deep sleep. He was pleased to note that the Rohypnol had done its work.

He decided that she didn't need a booster shot, so he replaced the needle in its case. To get to this stage of his plan had cost him time and effort; he had even cancelled a trip to the Cape. At least his parents didn't quiz him too much about his decision not to travel with them.

He looked down at the sleeping figure – Marilyn in the prone position, out of her gourd, and at his mercy. It was all her fault and she had to be punished; so too the other party – that would come later. With deliberation he blew into his cupped hands and began to remove her clothing, item by item. Her body was unremarkable and he wondered what the secret of her attraction could possibly be. A spurt of anger went through him when he saw a familiar name tattooed on the inside of her thigh. He didn't notice the snow that drifted down outside his window.

Some weeks earlier, before the snow came, Anthony was worried. His long-time girlfriend,

Emma, seemed distracted. They sat together in the Aula Max between lectures. Other students passed by, some giving nods and smiles in their direction. None stopped to chat because they knew that Anthony and Emma were an item, and, presumably needed privacy.

"Look Emma," he interjected, sensing that something had come between them in the past few months, "We used to be as close as..." Failing to find the right word, he raised two conjoined fingers.

"All I said was that you should pull your socks up, or change to Chemical Engineering." She knew he was drifting, and wanted him to be as driven and focused as she was.

As if reading her mind, he said, "Don't worry about me. I'll do OK. My folks aren't short of a buck..." He passed a cupped hand over the top of his head, massaging the close-cropped hair.

"That's hardly the point, Anthony..." She shifted uneasily. Yes, they had been close as kids, playing on the beach together, having slumber parties, the whole nine yards. But recently she sensed something about him, a change of some sort that undermined his former appeal. Maybe college didn't suit him.

"We all know that you won scholarships. Not all of us can be as smart as you..."

Was that a compliment, she wondered, or was there a sneer in his voice? "I worked hard for everything," she answered truthfully. She fell silent as another student paused to drink from a nearby fountain. She looked at her phone. "Must dash. Time for my lecture in orthopaedics." She rose and patted down her skirt.

"We wouldn't want you to miss that."

She ignored the sarcasm and made to go.

"I'll call by later," he said to her departing back.

"OK." She said over her shoulder.

He went downstairs to his locker and, despite the presence of a number of people, snorted a line of coke off the top shelf. Later, he sauntered into the Oak Canteen and as he sipped a black coffee, Marilyn joined him. She offered him half her cookie which he declined.

"Listen Mar, you're a good friend of Emma... Is there anything bothering her?" He hadn't meant to be so blunt and put it down to the coke.

"Why would you ask me that?" Marilyn looked at him closely over the top of her tinted spectacles while passing a hand through a hank of wavy hair.

"You know her well."

"I wouldn't say that," she replied carefully. "Anyway, I can't help you."

"But..." He didn't go on. Marilyn was typical of her Gender Studies group, he thought, prejudiced against men unless they were gay and / or black. She had always been polite to him but he sensed that she would never confide in him and, no doubt, she resented his straight white male privilege. He had no idea that she and

Emma had begun an affair a month earlier. He made his excuses and left. Back in the frat house he scanned the noticeboard for messages. A friend passed by.

"How's it hanging, Dude?"

"Low and free. Down to the knee." He ran up the stairs and into his room where he snorted another line and lay on his bed, gazing at some interesting hair-cracks in the plaster of the ceiling.

He went over to Emma's quarters that evening. As he passed down a corridor, he saw Marilyn getting into the elevator, and answered her half-hearted wave with a nod. When he entered the room, he found Emma sitting at her desk with several textbooks and a laptop open in front of her.

She removed her headphones and turned in her cushion-padded swivel chair to face him. "I think the snow is going to get worse," she observed. "The hills are almost invisible."

He sat at a small dining table. "I think we should cut to the chase."

She nodded and stroked a strand of fair hair back from her face and looped it around an ear. Her earnest face showed that she anticipated and understood what was on his mind.

"Well I mean … how close are we now?" he blurted it out. There was no point beating around the bush. As kids they were hand-in-glove. He knew she had enjoyed playing in his house which was so much bigger than hers and had its own designated playroom. They went to the beach together in his Dad's capacious Mercedes. It was always Emma and himself and he assumed that they, as a couple, would go on forever. It was a natural continuation. Their fathers had trained as accountants together and even though his Dad followed an entrepreneurial route and became very wealthy as a venture capitalist, it made no difference to the kids.

"Anthony, we'll always be friends, best friends I hope."

He went on tilt. "But not more than that?"

She turned her chair around to face him squarely. "It's hard to explain. When we were younger, we had no wider perspective. When you grow up you begin to see the world differently... I'm sure you've experienced that..."

"Oh, come on ... we're made for each other. And we weren't kids when we began sleeping together. That lasted for over a year if you remember." A harsh note had entered his voice.

"Anthony, that was never going to last." She had once shared his vision of both of them being paired for life but she gradually realised that there were flaws in him that became more apparent as they both grew up. That was when fissures appeared. Maybe it had something to do with his family's growing fortune. The fact was that Anthony now shirked responsibility for most things, and she knew he did coke. Being lazy, he would probably envy her work ethic, which was now an integral part of her nature. If she became successful in her chosen field, it was more than likely that he would come to resent her. But maybe she didn't have to tell him all of this; there was a better way, also true, which might minimise conflict and hurt feelings.

"I have to tell you…" she began slowly. "It's only fair…"

"Another guy. Oh Christ, who?" He crouched instinctively as if expecting a blow to the guts.

"No, it's more complicated than that."

"Everything has to be complicated with you."

She fell silent and after a while he grunted an apology.

"I said we grew apart. I probably changed more than you." She was preparing to shoulder the blame.

"You got smarter than me. I accept that. And I'm sure you'll be more successful."

"There's something else." She drew in a long preparatory breath. "I was never fully sure about my sexuality for a long time. I couldn't believe when the penny dropped. There had been a lot of role-playing – "

"What are you talking about?" He craned forward, resting his elbows on the table.

"For a while I thought I was Bi but now I know that I'm gay."

He gave a short bark of laughter. "You a Lessie? Pull the other one."

She looked at him steadily. "It's true, Anthony. That's how it is. That's who I am. And there's nothing either of us can do about it."

He stood and paced the small room, grinding a fist into the palm of the other hand. "I don't believe this... We slept together..."

"I put an end to that if you remember." She recalled that when her ardour had cooled, he had become more aggressive in bed. That had served only to accelerate the break-up.

"Oh, I remember all right." That much was true. At the time he felt he must have been inadequate in some way. He stopped and looked at her. "How can you be sure if you haven't tried it ... if you haven't had a gay relationship?"

"I have," she said quietly.

He moved closer to her. "Who?"

There was no good reason not to tell him. "Marilyn..."

"I just saw her in the corridor." His eyes grew wide. "Was she here?" He looked towards the sleeping area, at the crumpled quilt and sheets and the scattered soft toys. "Jesus Christ." He was betrayed by his best friend. It was corny, yes, but still painful.

Later that night, when high, he told some of his frat buddies what had happened, trying to boast about the fact that he had ruined his girlfriend for other men. They used his maudlin show of misery as an excuse to indulge in alcohol and their drugs of choice. They were brothers-in-arms after all.

After the rape, Marilyn went into herself and allowed depression to take hold. Emma couldn't get her to talk but she knew her friend and lover had suffered some dreadful trauma. They met several times in the safe space for women and gays. Over a few days the story came out piecemeal. When Emma demanded to know who the attacker was, Marilyn began to weep again.

"Tell me, Sweetheart," Emma urged gently, holding the shuddering body of her partner. She didn't hear the name at first and when she realised it was Anthony, she felt the floor move under her feet, and had to sit down.

"That's why I didn't go to the police," Marilyn said through her tears.

"But you have to report it," Emma said firmly. "It was a cruel and calculated crime. It makes no difference that he was a friend, or that we were together once." She could hardly believe that Anthony had gone this far. He had suddenly become a stranger to her. What on earth had motivated him? Was it some form of sick revenge?

The next day, Marilyn, accompanied by Emma, reported the crime to the police. A female police officer interviewed Marilyn for several hours, after which a doctor examined her. The pattern of bruises, still not faded, were consistent with penetrative rape. Depositions were signed and filed.

The Deputy District Attorney had no hesitation in prosecuting the case. He took a pragmatic view. Marilyn would be a good witness and would stand up to the defence. The fact that she had never had affairs with men would be a definite plus, since there could be no question of her having led him on. And then it was far more than date rape or a belated Me-Too sort of accusation; a drug had been used, and the accused was known to traffic in drugs at least for his personal use. There could be no doubt that the crime was premeditated and planned down to the last detail.

Emma contacted Anthony several times and asked him what he hoped to achieve by such a vile and despicable act. He denied it each time and told her to leave him alone. But she could see that he was shaken, and she noticed that he was high on each occasion. The last time she went to his rambling Cape Cod-style house, knowing that his parents had gone to the Bahamas to avoid the snow. She sat opposite him in front of a log fire and pressed him for answers.

"Why did you do it? You know, you're going to go down…"

"Oh, not that shit again. Emma, you really don't know me at all." A maid came in from the conservatory and he waved her away. "Marilyn was pissed out of her skull at that party. She mistook me for someone else – assuming of course that she *was* raped."

"You should plead guilty…"

"Why would I do that? And, by the way, I could sure tell you some stories about your precious Marilyn. She's not as innocent as you think she is."

"Cut it out … I thought I did know you once. But not now. You've become a sneaky, entitled bastard."

"Fuck you too."

Emma stormed out and sat into her VW Beetle fuming. She tried to console herself with the thought that justice would be done when the trial came to court.

By this time the news of the indictment had spread over the campus. Marilyn stayed away to avoid comments and what she perceived to be sniggers. Anthony spent most of the time in the frat house, where he told anyone who would listen how he was being scapegoated. His friends gathered round him as if protecting a member of the fraternity.

In early spring Marilyn called to her room; after some cajoling Emma brought her to bed where they made love for the first time since the rape. Afterwards Emma held her tightly for a long time, listening to the exalted rhythm of her heart. Marilyn eventually detached and sat upright.

"I have something to tell you."

"What is it, Lover?"

"Don't be mad at me."

"Of course not." Emma sat up too and put her arm around her friend.

"Well, I've decided, on balance, to … withdraw the charges."

"What?" It took Emma a while to process this shocking news. Then she asked for reasons, which were not immediately forthcoming.

"Marilyn, it's an open and shut case. You can't stop now. Look, I know it will be hard on you, but I'll be with you every step of the way." She hugged her and caressed her wavy hair.

"I've decided," Marilyn said in the firmest voice she could muster.

"Wait now, has there been some kind of pressure…?"

"No… Look, Emma, it is a strong case but there's always an element of risk. If I lost, my reputation would be destroyed … and my family humiliated."

"You won't lose." Emma felt there was something missing. "Think of all the other women out there who would benefit." What was she not getting? There had to be something else.

"As far as I know, the DDA could still prosecute the case."

"Not without me as a witness."

What was going on? Emma wondered. She didn't let up, though it was hard to interrogate her partner who had been through so much. After much probing, Marilyn admitted tearfully that she had accepted an offer made by Anthony's family. Emma was shocked to the core and pleaded with her to reject the settlement.

"Marilyn, you're still traumatised. "You can't let him away with this. What if he does it again?" She wasn't convinced that he would do it to anyone else. It seemed to her that it was a one-off act of vengeance. "There's a principle involved." This was her last throw of the dice.

"I can't afford principles … not like you."

"What does that mean? My family doesn't have money."

"But you have brains."

"Jesus, I can't believe you're doing this."

"I've decided." Marilyn moved to touch her cheek and, to her shame, Emma backed away. She realised at that moment that Anthony had achieved exactly what he wanted. He had taught both of them a lesson they would not forget and, as a bonus, ruined their relationship. It felt as if her world was breaking down.

AND IT BEFELL

THE UNFORTUNATE FARMER whom John had hit with his car on that dark road in Leitrim didn't have a light on his bike or even a reflector. In court his widow hadn't denied it. The police had, in any case, examined the bike after they pulled it out of the ditch. Even the prosecution was half-hearted, especially when it emerged that the farmer had been returning from the pub where he usually had four or five pints of stout. John had not been drinking, and he had a spotless driving record for over fifteen years.

No one was in much doubt that the case would be dismissed. But still, when the judge gave this widely expected verdict, John felt his knees go weak. The last month had been a nightmare.

"...a tragic accident," the judge added, and extended his sincere condolences to the widow and the two children. They had had their day in court and that was all they were going to get.

Outside the courthouse, Ruth embraced John. "I knew it'd be thrown out. I knew it." She hugged him closely. "All those months worrying... It's over at last. Finally..."

The daylight hurt his eyes. There were a few journalists around but they weren't intrusive – an acquittal was not the stuff of front-page headlines even on a slow news day.

When he went back to work his medical

colleagues gave him a warm reception. The staff of the hospital congratulated him, as if he had won some sort of trophy. Many of the doctors, had been the victims of litigation in the past and they were glad that John had beaten the rap his first time out – even though it had not been a medical suit. The Consultant put his arm around John's shoulder, "I can imagine what you've been through, John, but it's all over now."

It was all a bit cloying but they meant well. During the preparations for the court case some of his colleagues had distanced themselves from him in a subtle way, as if unable to believe fully in his innocence. Now that the verdict was out, they treated him warmly, as if apologising for their earlier suspicions.

Ruth suggested going out for a celebratory dinner but John said he'd prefer a quiet evening at home. That was fine with her, and they both cobbled together a potluck meal from the contents of the fridge. She reminded him a number of times that the nightmare was over.

Except that it wasn't over. Not for him. He relived the events of that night in minute detail, usually when he was alone but sometimes when he was in company or even doing his rounds. He would go over the seconds before and after the sickening impact. Nightmares weren't too difficult to cope with. More difficult by far were those agonising daydreams that started with a bout of nausea as if he were on the point of throwing up. Sometimes bile came to his throat and he did retch.

Ruth knew what he was going through and she did her best to help him.

"John, it was an accident. An accident. You were unlucky … in the wrong place at the wrong time. The court decided completely in your favour. You're innocent, free…"

"God, if this is freedom…" He wondered if he would ever come to terms with it. Those daydreams were becoming more frequent rather than less…

"For Christ sake, John, let it go…" The more insidious his doubts became, the more aggressive her rebuttals grew. He was grateful to have her on his side, but he sometimes wondered if she protested just a little too much. She certainly had no interest in unpicking the legal verdict…

A narrow road, and a filthy night. The windscreen wipers flapped back and forth at top speed. When it started to rain and he found himself on the minor road, he slowed his driving to suit the conditions. That was certainly true. He had been overtaken by several cars and had, in his mind, berated the unknown drivers for their recklessness. They were probably locals who knew the road better than he did, but still they were taking excessive risks.

He wasn't in a hurry and was in good time for the meeting in Carrick. The lights of the car, on high beam, raked the tall hedge on the left-hand side and created a reasonably bright path on the unmarked road for him to follow. Once, he saw the startled, phosphorescent eyes of a small animal that broke cover and streaked across the road, disappearing into the hedge opposite, probably a fox. John had slowed the car to let the fox pass but he didn't have to brake too hard – further testimony to his careful driving.

He remembered that strange feeling of being alone in a dark world, sitting in a metal box, surrounded by the immensity of night.

An oncoming car flashed him. That was unusual. John normally dimmed his lights well in advance, without having to be reminded. Why the lapse this time? He must have been absorbed by something...

Often, the sheer tedium of driving induced a trancelike state. How many times had he driven home to Killiney on automatic pilot? If Ruth had asked him whether a particular set of traffic lights had been red or green he wouldn't have known. Driving could become as automatic as a reflex; not engaging the mind at all. All drivers experienced that, though not all would say so. In any case, who could prove that automatic driving was more dangerous than the more self-aware kind? Was there experimental data on that? He doubted it.

He deeply regretted the death of the farmer and the effect that was bound to have on his widow and children. Why had he been chosen as the instrument of the tragedy? How many fatal accidents had he read about in the papers without turning a hair? He hadn't been involved in those.

This was different. Some kind of Fate had capriciously selected him. Or was that too easy? Too easy by far.

For some reason, after being flashed by the other car, he hadn't put his headlights back on full beam. However, the dipped lights of the car were quite adequate for visibility. He had thought so at the time, but had he assumed that nobody would be out on such a filthy night? What else might he have assumed?

For days, these thoughts occupied his mind. Sometimes they came in sequence as if on a loop; at other times they came in no particular order. After two more weeks he decided he had to go back to revisit the scene.

"Why on earth would you do that?" Ruth inquired of him. "This is some kind of compulsive behaviour. You're really beginning to worry me, John."

"There may be something I've forgotten, Ruth."

"So what if there is? Suppose you *belched* before the impact? Would that make you guilty? Of course not. The judge had all the facts he needed to make a clear-cut decision about your innocence. Just accept it, for God's sake. Even if you'd had a bout of sneezing or an epileptic fit would that have made it your fault? No, it would not. Come on, John, put it behind you." She put her arms around him and rubbed her palms up and down his back as if to massage in the words, and he was almost convinced by her – not just by her argument but also by her obvious passion. She was a great person to have in his corner.

But the following week was worse than ever. On Wednesday when Ruth went to visit her mother, John got into the car and headed north on the M50. It was a wet night, just like the one when the accident happened. The only difference was that there was a crescent moon which silvered the wet road from time to time. This should have made driving easier but somehow it did not – maybe because the light came in intermittent flashes through the tallest trees. He made good time and after an hour or so turned onto the minor road that he had so often dreamt about. He remembered the high unruly hedges, the muddy shoulders of the unmarked road and the shadows of overhanging trees. Here, the random flashes of moonlight became unsettling. His nerve began to go and he drove very slowly. Some kind of farm vehicle passed him, spraying his car with mud and grit from the surface of the road. He turned off the radio which he hadn't really been listening to. For one awful second he thought he saw the dark figure of a cyclist up ahead. He slowed down even more and realised that the spectre was a combination of shadows and his imagination. The car radio… Something came to him about the radio. He pulled into a gateway and stopped…

On the fateful night, he had switched the radio on at some point and become interested in a political discussion; he remembered marvelling at the evasiveness and platitudes of the contributions. Some scandal or other. Which one, he couldn't recall. They all merged into one great big scandal. He was a voyeur, enjoying the discomfort of these venal people as they protested their innocence or claimed some kind of executive deniability: "Had no knowledge of the events, good, bad or indifferent. There was no official report as such – only an aide memoire. Not a scintilla of evidence. No conflict of interest or favours given. I didn't interrupt you. There was no formal meeting on that date…" John remembered the artifice that lay behind the words. The truth could be avoided in so many ways.

Why was the electorate so gullible and docile? He felt queasy but was fascinated at the same time. It was like watching snakes wriggle in a cesspit. More detailed recollections came to him.

Without taking his eyes off the road, he had groped towards the radio to turn up the volume but hit the wrong button and lost all sound. He had looked down briefly at the controls, which were just barely visible in the greenish light reflected from the dashboard. His car didn't have radio controls on the steering wheel. Even though the car had slowed it would have been dangerous to concentrate for much longer on the radio. He had raised his eyes and watched the road. There was a bend coming up. He waited until he rounded the bend and registered the new stretch of road in his mind's eye.

Then he fumbled again at the radio but had lost his marker. He glanced down for a split second. No more than that. Then looked up. Suddenly a shape in front ... Jesus, a man on a bicycle! John braked and swerved. Went into a skid. Tried to steer away. No good. Then the sickening thud that he would never forget.

He had fought a sudden urge to drive away. For a moment he almost persuaded himself that nothing had happened. But he brought the car to a halt and walked back. Every step filled him with dread. He stumbled over a wheel of the bike which was mangled. As his eyes became accustomed to the dark he saw the man lying motionless in the ditch. He sank to his knees in the wet grass and felt for a pulse in the man's neck. Maybe it was just concussion. But there was no pulse, and John knew immediately that the neck was broken. The man was dead. By his hand...

Sitting behind the wheel in the gateway, tears came to his eyes. This was not the memory he wanted. He hoped for something that would make him *feel* innocent deep inside. But it was not to be.

In court the lawyers had dealt with all of the major objective aspects: alcohol levels, past records, weather conditions, adequacy of warning lights, etc. But no one asked him about the imponderables, such as how well he had been concentrating on his driving. No one elicited the small facts either, like fiddling with the radio. The law had no finesse; it was blunt, binary. There were so many degrees of innocence and guilt it could not cope with. Should he volunteer this information now? Hardly; that was not how the legal game was played.

John did, however, volunteer the information to Ruth one evening after dinner. She got to her feet and delivered a vehement response, as if she had been half expecting to hear what he had just said. "Don't ever, ever repeat any of that rubbish to another living soul. I can't believe you went back there... You shouldn't be entertaining these thoughts at all. They are completely and utterly beside the point. I'm beginning to think you have a martyrdom complex. Or maybe it's a Christ thing; you want to atone for the sins of the world. You fiddled with the radio ... so what?"

"That was a willed decision on my part ... not a reflex like sneezing..."

"So now we're getting into a discussion of free will. I just don't believe this. Think of your own family for a change. For God's sake, the man had no light of any sort on his bicycle. He was wearing a dark suit. The amazing thing is that he survived as long as he did on that road, coming home from the pub late at night, year after year. He was an accident waiting to happen. You could not have avoided him. You braked, swerved, skidded, did everything that was humanly possible. You put your own life at risk. Now you want to kill yourself by inches. Why not punish yourself for the starving children of the world? Put it out of your mind. It happened. It was an accident. It's over." She paused for breath and then shouted, "What do you think an accident is, for God's sake?"

BUCK-PASSING WITH HEART

THERE WAS A PROBLEM with the drain. It backed up at frequent intervals and Terence had to get the Dyno-rod Sewer Doctors out on an emergency basis. It was costing a fortune, the problem kept recurring, and Terence had to contact the 'pox doctors', as he called them, almost every second week. He and his wife, Ruth, eventually hit on the idea of getting the Local Authority drain men out on *nixers* – cash only, no questions asked. That was cheaper, of course, but after each *rodding,* the drain would start backing up again; sewage would leak out of the manhole and spread all sorts of unmentionable matter over the lawn and flower beds in their garden.

The postman, who was also the local oracle, helpfully vouched for the fact that the previous owners of the house had had dreadful problems with the same drain which, truth be told, had put the local plumber's kids through college. Ruth was becoming agitated; the mere mention of a *soil pipe* caused her distress. Terence reassured her and said he would fix things for once and for all. This was man's work – exactly what a husband was expected to bring to a marriage. But this was before he met the Inspector of Drains who worked for the Local Council.

"I don't know." The Inspector of Drains (IOD) shook his head. "I don't like the look of that gully trap." The sharp intake of breath was pure caricature, as was the sorrowful grimace that followed.

"What's wrong with it?" Terence inquired.

"I can't say."

"You don't know?"

"I do know, but it's not a Council matter."

"What?"

"I can't tell you because it's not a Council matter."

Terence could hardly believe his ears, but he gradually learned that since the trap was in his garden, it was not a matter for the Council or the IOD. This was an aspect of intellectual property rights he had not come across before. He had always assumed that IPRs applied to computer apps, pharma products and surgical instruments, but now he realised that drains were no different. Diagnosis of a malfunctioning drain on private property would not be made by a public official. There was no help forthcoming, not even advice. He was on his own.

In the weeks that followed he did a substantial amount of research and discovered that legally the Council did not have to take any responsibility for his manhole. However, a pipe went from his manhole into another one outside his gate and the latter was definitely on public property. Who was to say that the problem didn't *start* in the *public* manhole; if that was blocked then the sewage would back up the pipe into the manhole in his garden. What was the *ultimate* cause of the problem, the First Cause? He was brought back over the years to his encounters with Thomistic philosophy.

To confuse matters even more, another question arose: who had responsibility for the pipe joining the two manholes, the private one and the public one? Maybe he had responsibility for the section that ran through his garden, but surely the Council was in charge of the section which ran under the public road? The foot or so that was directly under his wall or curtilage was a legal minefield that could keep lawyers employed for several years. In any event there had to be metaphysical difficulties in deciding which section of a pipe caused a blockage. The actual detritus – or sclerosis to take a medical analogy – might be located in one specific section, but the offending matter could have come from the *other* section of pipe – or artery. The clot might be moving. He doubted if the IOD was really interested in trying to disentangle these complexities.

"It's a very tricky area," Terence would say to Ruth sometimes after their evening meal when the kids had been put to bed.

"I don't care about legal niceties. I just want it fixed, permanently. No more leaks. Please just get it fixed. We have the children to think about." There was something tragic in her tone. Maybe *he* could afford to dabble in philosophical and legal speculation but *she* had a family to look after. She no longer let the kids play in the garden and she, herself, who had planted many fine shrubs, such as Veronica, Berberis and Cotoneaster, refused to do any more gardening. Talk of the Ebola virus, E coli and superbugs that learned how to outsmart antibiotics, was in the air. Hospitals frequently reported outbreaks of vomiting flu and MRSA. The world had become a dangerous place.

They both had bad memories of a holiday in southern Italy where the hotel they stayed at wasn't quite finished and there was that faint smell of sewage wherever they went. The best thing about that holiday was the moment they got on the plane home.

"Will do." He promised, still having reason to hope. Or, more accurately, because there was no compelling reason to abandon hope at that early stage.

The next time it backed up, there was considerable overflow on his side of the wall; an entire crop of snapdragons was wiped out and neighbours and passers-by had to hold handkerchiefs to their noses. Terence got a Council crew out on a *nixer*. They rodded the drain, using six lengths of rod extension, as well as an instrument known as a ferret.

"That means the blockage is *outside* the wall," Terence said triumphantly. "It's in *your* section of the pipe which is under the public road."

"Oh no," one of the two crew members said. "It's still your pipe. It doesn't become ours until *after* it reaches our manhole."

Relieved that the blockage was removed, Terence didn't argue the point and he slipped a twenty-euro note into a pocket of each of the boiler suits, with an extra twenty for the gaffer.

In answer to Ruth's question, he said he thought the problem was solved.

"Permanently?" She burped a baby on her shoulder; a little stream of lumpy off-white dribble appeared.

"Oh yes." He added a *Please God* under his breath. He felt like a pioneer who had to make the log cabin presentable for his delicate, citified wife unprepared for the rough-and-tumble of the frontier.

Ten days later it backed up again. Mayhem! Ruth threatened to move out to a hotel with the children. He called Dyno-rod Sewer Doctors this time. As the surgeon-plumber was pulling on his heavy-duty rubber gloves (incongruously pink ones) he said he knew the area well and asked Terence if he realised what he was up against.

"What are you telling me?" Terence felt weak.

"You're bound to get blockages in this location."

"Why? For God's sake why?"

"The gradient is all wrong." The plumber brought him out on to the public road and pointed. "That manhole up there at the corner is over fifty metres away and it is higher than your one. Water doesn't run uphill, you know."

"Good God." Terence felt his extremities go numb. It was as if nature and physics were conspiring against him. He couldn't win against such powerful opponents.

"You don't have to be Einstein to figure out what the problem is. I suppose the Council lads have been stringing you along? That drain has kept them in beer money for years. Long before your time."

"Oh, God." Terence held his head, feeling a migraine coming on. "Maybe the Council doesn't know about the gradient?"

The plumber laughed loudly. "And my Granny doesn't know how to suck eggs. Of course they know it. They use that trap up there as a sink. They have to pump it out every week."

"Wha-a-at? They pump it out ... every week?" None of the officials had mentioned that to him and no one had referred to the gradient.

Terence lay in wait in a parked car. After about two hours he saw a yellow vehicle approach and stop. Two crewmen in hi-vis jackets got out and inserted a large-bore hose into the manhole at the corner. The pumping went on continuously for a good half hour. There was no doubt about it: If they went to all that trouble every week then it meant they knew all about the gradient. It also meant that they did take responsibility for all of the pipe under the public road. Terence was shaken by what he had seen but pleased that his research had yielded such an important discovery.

The IOD wasn't the least bit fazed when Terence pointed out the newly emerging facts.

"That changes nothing."

"It means that you, the Council, are responsible"

The IOD stroked an eyebrow and shook his head. "Not necessarily. Anyway, you'd have to prove that a blockage in our pipe was responsible for the blockage in your spur."

"But that has to be the case... Gravity alone..."

"Oh no. There's every reason to believe that our pipe is clear at all times. Therefore, the blockage is more than likely in your spur."

Terence gave his temples a fingertip massage to ease the throbbing in those large veins that carried blood from the heart to the brain, hopefully without any blockages.

"How do you know your pipe is clear?" he asked. "You can't prove it."

The IOD said that he could and would prove it, although he didn't have to. Legally, he didn't have to do anything.

The very next day a crew arrived with a fibre-optic device. They removed the manhole cover and ran the camera through the entire length of their pipe. They made a video of the inside of the pipe, every centimetre of its 50-metre length.

"You see?" The IOD pointed to the small monitor they had been staring at for fifteen minutes. "Completely clear. The problem is not in our section."

"You can't be sure of that," Terence said, thinking about the complexities of causation.

"Yes, I can. There was no build-up of matter in our section."

"You love your work, don't you?" Terence bit his tongue just in time. Instead, he asked if they might run the camera along his spur, just about two metres. If they could diagnose the problem correctly he could have it fixed for once and for all. The IOD and the crewmen exchanged glances; they thought that Terence's request was a joke. Did he still not understand the difference between public and private? He could rent a fibre-optic ferret for about 300 euros.

"But you have one right there," Terence said, stabbing with his finger as he pointed repeatedly at the device they had just used.

"That's Council property. We can't use that on private property." The IOD ordered the crewmen to put the camera back on the truck. As the exhaust fumes melted away, Terence looked darkly at the manhole cover which had been replaced. He began to feel afraid, realising the full extent of the power wielded by an inspector of drains. Money was power but shit was omnipotent. It occurred to him that people who worked for the Council were a different species. People like Terence paid their wages through property taxes and other charges, but that did not imply any form of reciprocation or responsibility. The Council species seemed to hate the resident species, and treated them as hostile aliens whose mere existence was an affront.

The next time the blockage occurred, Ruth made good on her promise, gathered up the children and moved into a hotel. Fearful of losing his family, Terence got his Dyno-rod pox doctor out on an emergency basis, completely disregarding the cost. He needed someone to talk to; it was as much therapy as plumbing.

The plumber made sympathetic noises as he listened to the story. It didn't surprise him in the least that the Council refused to video his spur.

"Fifty notes would've done it," he said.

"A bribe?" Terence realised what a simpleton he must appear to these men whose lives revolved around drains and run-off and faecal matter.

When they agreed a price – Terence didn't even try to bargain – the Dyno-rod man made his own video of Terence's spur. They looked at the screen together.

"How bad is it?" Terence asked.

"Bad enough. It's an old earthenware pipe and it's cracked here and there. See the roots of that apple tree? Roots are a killer…"

"I'll cut it down." Although Ruth and the

kids were very fond of the old apple tree, Terence was ready to sacrifice it without a second thought. First things first. He'd cut down an entire orchard for the sake of his family.

"But the real problem is subsidence. At the point where your pipe enters the gully there's definite slippage. Look. You can see there where your pipe is out of alignment. So there's a kind of lip. That's where the matter gets caught and that's where it piles up."

"Please fix it." A tremor had come into Terence's voice; the euphemism, *matter*, chilled him to the bone. "Please." He wanted his family back. He wanted a shit-free environment. It wasn't asking a lot. He could get a loan from the bank if he had to. A normal life, that's all he wanted. "Please fix it." He suddenly realised why plumbers earned so much: consumers were terrified of shit.

The plumber went over the options. One involved flooding the pipe with a special high-tech chemical solution which would fill the cracks and even out the lip. Another was to replace the pipe; that would mean knocking down and rebuilding the perimeter wall. But there were no guarantees.

"What are you saying?" Terence began to panic. "That we'll end up with a … a … septic tank in the garden?"

"It could come to that," the plumber said. "Even if we straighten out your pipe there's still the problem of the gradient. The run-off from that pipe has to go somewhere. The Council would have to dig up the whole road. Do you see them doing that? Just to help you?"

"No." Terence wiped away a tear. He was surrounded by evil. The Local Authority was worse than Kafka's Castle. Was there some legal action he could take? A court case would be dragged out for five or more years and lawyers charged more than plumbers for work of less consequence. He wanted his family back now. And he wouldn't lobby a politician. Never. Never. Never. He rummaged through his wallet and offered the contents. "There's almost a hundred there. That's just for your best advice. What should I do? What would you do?"

The plumber looked at him. "There is one way. But it'll cost…"

"Fuck the cost." Shit was a form of corruption anyway. It was being borne in on him, by various Tribunals of Inquiry into political graft, that the country was run on faecal matter, that inexpensive and eminently renewable fuel.

And that was how it came to pass that Terence installed a powerful electric pump in his manhole. It was so powerful it pumped everything out through 'his' pipe into the manhole on the public road. Because of the poor gradient there continued to be blockages of course, but they occurred in the Council's pipe and frequently the raw sewage seeped out of the Council's manholes on to the public road. It could not do otherwise since Terence's pump blasted it out and away from his garden. In the event, the legalities didn't matter – nor did the fact that Terence's pump was wasteful of energy – public opinion was against the Council who had to come each time to clear up the mess on the road.

They often tried to get Terence to remove the pump which was making their lives difficult, and each time he would enjoy telling them that the pump was on his property, was his responsibility and was none of their business. By shifting the blockage from his section to theirs he had also passed the buck. That was the unkindest cut and they hated him for it.

Sometimes when he couldn't sleep at night he would wander down the garden to his manhole and listen for a while to the reassuring throbbing of the pump as it continued to shift the burden with the regularity of a heartbeat.

Some fifteen years later, a mere moment in Council time, the authorities did dig up the road and improve the gradient. And, though he didn't need it anymore, Terence still kept the pump going. Having saved his marriage and family, if not indeed his life, he regarded it as a sort of second heart.

DON'T GO ON

SHE SAT GRIMLY in the stationary car, a canary yellow Yaris, her hands resting on the steering wheel. There was no movement of her head even when people shouted at her and kicked the car in frustration. The traffic jam that had formed behind her car snaked around the Green and was about a half mile long, and growing all the time. The air was filled with a klaxon chorus of nonstop honking reminiscent of a truckers' blockade in any French city.

"For Christ's sake, move, woman!" an irate taxi driver shouted at her. There was no reaction; she stared sphinx-like ahead as if completely unaware of the chaos she was causing. Or indifferent to it.

A few moments earlier someone had suggested that she might have had a seizure or a stroke but closer inspection by the taxi driver and his posse of helpers had ruled that out. Nor was the car broken down; the engine was idling nicely.

"Where's the bloody Guards when you need them?" The taxi driver appealed to all and sundry and the clouds in the overcast sky. A tall trucker shook his head in despairing agreement, although he seemed to be more resigned to the oddities of human nature.

A woman shopper who'd just come out of Dunnes Stores paused on the footpath, appraised the situation for a while and then went to satisfy her curiosity. Having peered into the Yaris at the impassive profile of its owner, she asked her if she was all right. No reply.

"Maybe she's gone cataplexic," the woman shopper suggested.

"Not at all." The taxi driver wouldn't hear of it. "We even thought she might have gone into labour but she's as thin as a lath."

A black-suited undertaker who had abandoned his hearse fifty yards back pushed forward and carried out his own appraisal.

"I wonder if ... it could be ... you know ... like..."

"No, it's not," the woman shopper shouted at him.

"How do you know?"

"Shut up. It's none of your business."

The undertaker disagreed, pointing out that it was indeed his business since he had to call at a house on the South Circular Road within the hour to "effect a remains removal." The bereaved had hired him because of the quality of service he provided. His reputation was on the line. The normally taciturn trucker also spoke up, informing the woman that he had a load of lumber to deliver to a mill in Dundalk before five o'clock.

Because he had only seen her profile he couldn't be sure, but she seemed vaguely familiar to him.

The taxi driver approached the Yaris again in

his self-appointed role as spokesman.

"We don't know what your problem is, Missus, but you'll have to move on." He became more conciliatory. "We drive for a living. We could all lose our jobs if you don't move on."

The woman wound down the window an inch and, without looking at him, said, "I'm not going to break the law."

The taxi driver exchanged bewildered glances with his fellow delegates, one of whom touched a fingertip to his temple and rolled his eyes.

"What law?"

She nodded towards the continuous white line in the middle of the street. The gesture meant nothing to the taxi driver who opened out his hands as if beseeching heaven for inspiration. The trucker stepped forward to give his interpretation. The woman couldn't pull into the side because of double-parked cars which left a very narrow channel. To pass those cars she would have to put a wheel over the continuous white line that bisected the street. This she was not prepared to do since, strictly speaking, it would be breaking the law.

Armed with this information the taxi driver returned to the window, which remained open an inch. After a tense exchange it seemed as if the trucker had hit the nail on the head. The taxi driver had another pow-wow with his tribal council and then returned to the slightly open window which was beginning to resemble, in his mind, the screen in a confession box, dividing penitent from confessor.

"Look, we all have to break the law from time to time. For the greater good. Go on now. Be a good woman. Steer out a bit now and you'll be back on your own side of the road before you know where you are."

"I'm not going to break the law."

"But they're breaking the law." The taxi driver jerked his head in the direction of the double-parked cars. It wasn't that simple though and he knew it. The real problem was that the street wasn't wide enough for any parking. The Corporation Officials were to blame for the whole sorry mess. They hadn't a clue and couldn't care less. The whole city was gridlocked while the Corpo shuffled paper and red tape, drew their own pay and enjoyed their own underground parking facilities. Still, that was another day's work. The immediate priority was to shift this stubborn old Biddy.

She agreed with him about the double-parked cars and said they should be towed away. He concurred vigorously but pointed out that there was no sign of the Guards or of the towing firm used by the Corpo. He lowered his voice to a confidential, cajoling register, "Go on now. There's no Guards around. No one will know."

"I'd know."

He sighed and swore under his breath. She was obviously a fanatic of some sort. Or a Holy Mary with an overdeveloped conscience.

Possibly both. The Church had a lot to answer for. He began to lose confidence in his ability to deal with somebody like that.

The undertaker was becoming agitated. He had only twenty minutes left to get to the bereaved house and it was unthinkable for an undertaker to be late. It wasn't just a matter of business and reputation. Respect and courtesy came into it. Excuses were worthless and would only add insult to injury. As a class, the bereaved, according to his long experience, expected a top-notch service and could be extremely angry if that were not forthcoming. Their loss seemed to justify anger and rudeness.

"She's just acting the maggot," he said through compressed lips. Other frustrated drivers were joining the delegation, challenging their methods, urging them to try harder. "Get that hoor to move!" someone shouted. "Pull her outta the car!"

The taxi driver held up his hands, palms to the front, and tamped down the anger. He was in control and would think of something. He went into a huddle with his fellow delegates, nodded several times as the trucker whispered into his ear, and again approached the Yaris.

"If you get out for a minute, one of us will drive your car. For about fifty feet or so over the white line. Then you'll take over. That way you won't be breaking the law."

"I'm not insured for open driving."

"It'd only be for fifty feet or so."

"I'm not insured for that."

"So, are you going to sit here all day?" He was close to losing it; his voice had begun to tremble. Why had he put himself in this position? The cow was making him lose face in front of all these other road-users. He was too obliging for his own good. That was his problem; always trying to help people.

"If I have to. I have no legal alternative."

They considered phoning the Guards again, stressing the emergency nature of the blockage, but the consensus was against it for the simple reason that, technically speaking, the woman was legally correct. It was all the Corpo's fault, those damn traffic engineers daubing white lines everywhere. They knew nothing about what went on in the real world. The trucker had another idea. He had seen a car salesman in the traffic jam a short distance behind his truck.

"So?" The taxi driver demanded, not giving him a chance to finish.

"Car salesmen have open insurance. They can drive anything…"

A youngster on the fringes of the delegation was sent to get the car salesman who, upon arrival, confirmed that this was indeed the case. He seemed quite proud of the fact. He was whisked over to the Yaris and introduced to the woman by the taxi driver who also explained the man's special status and immunity.

"May I see your papers."

"Everyone knows car salesmen…"

"May I see your papers?"

"I don't have ... them ... on me... They're below in Carlow... The Yaris is a great little car..."

The taxi driver pulled him away, not wishing to be further humiliated. This woman wouldn't play ball with the Archangel Gabriel; she'd find some way to thwart him. The mood was darkening and the delegation was being pressured. If they couldn't find a solution they should stand aside and let others try. One man who had a delivery for a Florists said his carnations and tulips were already beginning to wilt. It just wasn't good enough and stronger action was clearly required. There were growls of assent and the taxi driver knew he would have to crank it up a notch if outright vigilantism was to be avoided. For his own sake, too, he had to get a result.

This time he brought a couple of stalwarts with him. The plan was to ease the woman out of the car and move the damn thing themselves. She could not possibly be accused of breaking any law and would probably be grateful. He tried the door handle of the Yaris. The door was locked but the woman knew what they were about.

"How dare you! If you lay a hand on my car or on me I'll sue you for assault and battery."

"Ah now, Missus, hold your horses. For God's sake, be reasonable..." He stopped in mid-sentence. Out of the corner of his eye he saw someone getting into one of the double parked cars. The man had just come out of a shop and was deploying parcels on the back seat. "Problem solved," the taxi driver said. But his prognosis was wrong and his relief shortlived.

The man with the parcels jerked his thumb at the woman, indicating that she would have to pass by to let him out. He did a double take when he saw her shake her head. She had no intention of crossing the white line just for him, especially since he was partly responsible for the whole mess. He got out of the car and joined the delegation. The situation was explained to him and he grew uneasy, knowing that if he couldn't get his car out there was a strong possibility he would be clamped.

"Proper order." The taxi driver had no sympathy for him. Only people who drove for a living were morally entitled to double-park. This gent was probably a civil servant who didn't even have to work for a living.

When it started to rain they all gave up and returned to their vehicles where they listened to the radio, read the newspaper, ate their sandwiches, talked on their mobiles. Eventually the Guards arrived and spoke for a while with the woman. She stated her case. They said it would be OK for her to cross the white line on this occasion; they would turn a blind eye. That wasn't the point at all, she responded. The law was the law. She was gravely disappointed in them. Their job was to enforce the law, not encourage people to break it. If they attempted to tow her car away she would sue them for gross dereliction of duty.

The Guards put up 'Diversion' signs to prevent the jam getting any longer; radio announcements also helped. At around 7pm the Corpo arrived. After much debate and pressure from the Guards, who wanted to get back to the barracks for their tea, the Corpo men painted out the white line. The woman put the Yaris in gear and moved on. The rest of the traffic, including the double-parked cars, followed her at a rate of knots, everyone breaking the speed limit until they caught up on the Yaris, which they overtook without a care for anyone's safety. The taxi-driver and the undertaker honked furiously as they passed her by. The trucker looked down at her from his lofty cab and wondered what had really happened to her.

Then it dawned on him. He had read about her in the newspaper. She had petitioned the courts for permission to end the life of her husband, who was dying from some dreadful, incurable illness. The courts had refused permission. She could hardly be blamed for becoming cynical about the law in general. He waved from the cab before turning left for the freedom of the motorway.

When most of the traffic had gone the Corpo restored the white line.

THE WRONG ADDRESS

SLEEP DIDN'T COME to Brendan Canavan until three-thirty, then he woke at eight, hollow-eyed, wondering why his wife, Maura, was already up. There were no kitchen sounds floating up from downstairs either. Odd that. His bemusement was not altogether unpleasant and he was about to let it ride – maybe even bask a little in it – when suddenly it resolved itself. His heart began to pound. He had to make a speech today. This day which he'd dreaded ever since the news of his daughter's engagement broke almost three months ago. It was now upon him. He couldn't stall or put the clock back.

The speech loomed up like an obstacle flung across his path; he hurtled towards it at dizzying speed. By late afternoon he would be on his feet addressing an audience of almost two hundred people. Already he could sense the blurred outline of myriad faces turning towards him, a horrible gell of frogspawn freezing his blood.

For the umpteenth time he began rehearsing the speech, a draft of which he'd secreted in his sock drawer: *Reverend Fathers, ladies and gentlemen... This is a wonderful day which we've all looked forward to ever since ... Sheila and Mark announced their engagement... Special thanks to Father Joe... Great pleasure in welcoming Mark into the family...*

A more confident man wouldn't have bothered to write out such obvious stuff but having done so, Brendan was somehow forced to learn it off; such was the tyranny of the written word. God, if he could only start with a joke. Laughter might give some relief; but even if he could think of a joke he mightn't be able to carry it off, and then where would he be? There was nothing as pathetic as a joke that falls flat.

He struggled out of bed, his head splitting. It could have been the worst imaginable hangover, if it weren't for the fact that he was a teetotaller. In the bathroom he went turgidly through his ablutions like a man under sentence, then, back in the bedroom, he sorted through the rented duds Maura had laid out for him. The starched collar of the shirt cut into his neck, and the rest of the ridiculous garb felt like a medieval apparatus of torture, like the iron maiden. It was going to be the trial of his life.

He made a token knock on Sheila's bedroom door.

"Don't come in," Maura sang out. "There's a pot of tea in the kitchen."

She was as good as her word except that the tea was stewed. He put the kettle on again and toyed with the idea of cornflakes until his stomach squirmed in protest. *Reverend Fathers, ladies and gentlemen … Father Joe… Mark…* Then what? He peeped at the script, which he'd transferred to his inside pocket. If only he could hide away in his office poring over his drawing board as he had done for the last twenty years. As a draughtsman he could work alone, concentrate on his designs, and wait for that secret rewarding moment when the lines and angles came together to capture exactly and define the original concept. Presentations and meetings he left to his more ambitious and self-assured colleagues, who were more than happy to unveil *his* drawings to clients. He had managed to avoid that part of the business with the cunning, indeed the brilliance, often displayed by people who couldn't read. Yes, he had put extraordinary energy into avoidance. But today would change the habit of a lifetime, to- day there would be no place to hide.

"When will the limousine be here?" Maura called downstairs as if it were an everyday occurrence.

"Ten," he threw back.

"Better not be late," she replied. He wasn't sure whether the admonition was directed at him, the chauffeur, or all of them put together. It was one of Maura's portmanteau warnings without which life could not function.

He poured a cup of tea and sat at the table, the idiotic tails of the rented suit hanging like panniers around the kitchen chair. He looked at his watch, extricating it from the folded cuff of the rented dress shirt. Nine-fifteen. He checked it against the clock on the wall over the spice-rack; nine-seventeen. Splitting the difference did not diminish the plenum of misery that lay over him.

His father used to berate him for being so self-conscious. It's just vanity, he used to say. What've you got to be vain about? The logic was tough but compelling. Brendan wasn't exactly bursting at the seams with credentials. He was plump and balding with a vacuous face scooped out of blancmange, and a silly little paunch which Maura sometimes patted – a homely uxorious gesture but one which also brought him to heel. So if there was nothing to be vain about, then what? A phobia – but that was just a name. If only he could forget about the damn speech until the moment came.

"I wouldn't be able to plan for it," he answered himself.

The other voice said, "Are you doing much planning now?"

"I suppose not." Brendan answered truthfully. "But I don't want the moment to sneak up on me. It would come as such a shock…"

"And what would happen?" The inner voice seemed faintly taunting.

"I … don't know… "He wrestled with his thoughts for a while and then came clean. "All right, dammit … if the moment arrived suddenly and I was caught off-guard, I might … I might … pass out…"

"So, by agonising over it now and for the next five or six hours you're going to avoid passing out? You think you can get the pain over now, in advance? It doesn't work like that. You suffer now *and* later."

Brendan of course knew that, but there was nothing he could do about it. A superb worrier like him was born, not made; before entering the birth canal he had acquired the need to placate some homage-seeking deity. Even when he ripped off a sheet of kitchen towel to give his shoes (his own, not rented) a final wipe, he was ruminating, preparing for the worst, picking at scabs which hadn't yet formed.

He was granted a momentary lull when Sheila was ushered into the kitchen for inspection in all her finery, stately as a Doric column, a Yeatsian dream-woman come of age. He stared at his daughter standing there, an epiphany in Carrickmacross lace and for once the draughtsman was struck by a beauty that went beyond symmetry.

"Ah, Sheila, you look…" he began, rubbing his hands on the morning coat.

"Doesn't she just," Maura said. "Careful," she added as he embraced her.

"Thanks, Dad." Sheila gave a little twirl. "Now let's get this show on the road." As she turned, Maura followed close behind, holding the train safely above the kitchen floor.

No sooner were they ensconced in the limousine than he was thrown back on himself, feeling more trapped than ever, being driven inexorably to the dreaded venue.

"Are you all right?" Maura inquired, almost daring him not to be. It was her day too and she wanted all her ducks in a row. Months of preparation had gone into it, megajoules of angst and energy. She clasped her hands. "This has to be the perfect day."

Further diminished by that non-negotiable demand, he sat on the edge of the jump-seat confronted by the distaff side whose expectations knew no bounds. The smell of perfume made him feel faint; powder particles seemed to congeal in his lungs.

He knew the unforgiving grip of perfection. As an altar boy, he had developed, for some unknown reason, a compulsion to pray perfectly. Each word of the prayer – Latin as well as English – had to be conceptualised, each syllable pronounced in the core of his heart. The prayer had to go out in a flawless stream like a seamless white ribbon; any lapse of concentration, however trivial, destroyed the whole fabric. If he failed on the last line, even the 'Amen', he had to start all over again. So many stops and starts, hours spent each day trying to achieve the integrity of the spheres. How did he ever grow up? Maybe he didn't.

A draughtsman had to be perfect too but that was easy, just a matter of measurement and the proper convergence of lines. Besides, there was always the blessed eraser, and the client wasn't God. "You'll wrinkle your suit." Maura brushed down his lapel. "What are you fiddling at anyway?"

"Oh, just some notes… in my pocket." He dropped the restless hand guiltily into his lap.

"Notes, as in money?"

"No. For the … speech." Even the mention of the word sent a tremor through him.

"What speech?"

He was aghast. How could she not know? "The father of the bride has to make a speech."

"Oh yes. I'd forgotten." She seemed a little ill at ease. If she'd forgotten that, was there anything else that had slipped her mind in the flurry of the last few days?

"What are you going to say?"

Christ, did she want to blue-pencil it for him?

"Don't go on too long, Dad," Sheila pleaded. "It's mainly a young crowd."

"Thanks," he muttered. But in a way he was grateful for her comment; it gave him a little running room, took some pressure off. During incessant rehearsals he'd managed to chop the damn speech down to about five minutes. But five minutes was, he knew, ample for calamity.

He looked across at the two women in his life and was staggered that, on this of all days, they could still evince such practicality. Sheila acted as if she were going to a party with her friends, while Maura was mainly concerned about the standard of catering. The sense of occasion pressed down on him; he felt press-ganged into a formal and complex ritual which allowed no latitude. He was inside a design.

And the groom was English, establishment material, not a spry Cockney or salt-of-the-earth Yorkshire lad. A decent polite young man, of course, who would do well by Sheila – indeed she could build a nest in his ear and rob it. But he was alarmingly poised and, like his family, moved with lazy grace through all the certain protocols of a ruling provenance. What he said seemed to Brendan to be but a minute fraction of what he thought; those faintly smiling English sentences had to be interpreted with caution.

"You didn't make a speech at our wedding," Maura remarked.

"Didn't I?" He lifted his brow in a parody of recall.

"Mark is going to say something," Sheila put in. "He read up on the etiquette."

"Well, maybe it's changed," Brendan said airily. Yes, he'd funked it back then and he'd funked it for the next quarter of a century. But now he had no choice.

Sweat broke out on his upper lip and his stomach heaved. It reminded him of the motion sickness that used to come over him in his Dad's old Ford Prefect, but he could hardly blame the limousine, which seemed to float on a cushion of air.

The traffic was lighter than they'd expected and in no time the church loomed up. The driver glanced at them through the rear-view mirror with an expression that prompted further instructions.

"We're too early," Maura said with some alarm, having taken a quick census of the rather small crowd in the churchyard. On a day like this punctuality was to be gauged by a head count rather than time.

"We can drop Dad off here and drive around for a while," Sheila suggested calmly. "Out you get, Dad."

Before he was unceremoniously dumped at the church gate he looked at them, these strangers. Then he fought his way through the back-slapping and banter of friends and relatives, hoping he could escape into the church and take his place in the pew. But he couldn't. He had to stand at the entrance until Sheila arrived.

Pumping his hand, his brother Jim said, "The Brits have already gone inside to say their prayers. The natives as usual are hovering around outside the door having a last fag."

"Oh God," Brendan groaned. Maura's census had been incomplete. It wouldn't have dawned on her that the groom's side had already gone into the church. He walked back to the gate and flagged down the limousine on its next lap.

"They're *inside*," he said in a strained voice. "Inside."

"Good." Maura stepped out of the car. With one hand she held onto her hat and with the other she carefully extricated Sheila. "I hope the bloody wind dies down." She calibrated Sheila's veil to the appropriate degree of mystery. "Before they start making the video."

"The what?" Brendan asked, a cold gelatinous substance spreading through his innards.

"The video. Everything's being filmed. Now, Sheila, shoulders back, head up. And smile. Your public awaits."

He would of course always regret that he went through the wedding ceremony in a daze. From the moment he led Sheila up the aisle and handed her by rote to the smiling Mark there was hardly a second in which he managed to escape the queasy off-beat rhythms of his heart. Trapped in the front pew, he sat, rose and knelt like clockwork, the spring rewinding itself after each movement into a tighter coil. At one point during the ceremony he had a mad desire to jump up and do something violent to shake himself out of that deadly cowed stupor. But of course he didn't. As they were filing out of the church he noticed a clergyman on the groom's side. A vicar, pastor, padre... what? He would have to amend the introduction to his speech. *Reverend Fathers, Padre...* What the hell was it? This problem occupied him all the way to the hotel, where he was momentarily diverted by the sight of the video cameraman nosing his way among the guests. "Great sermon, Father Joe," someone was saying. "A hard act to follow. You've set the bar very high."

He heard Maura's voice as if from a distance, but she was speaking to him.

"Please make an effort to enter into the spirit of the occasion. I just don't know what's got in to you..." Before he could respond she was whisked away for another G and T by some newly found relative. Oddly, he felt abandoned, and he nursed a lemonade among a group of whiskey-drinkers whose sudden bluster, after the solemnity of the church, overpowered him. They would be part of his audience; even if he could engage in idle chat with them now it might be giving hostages to fortune. He wondered if he should take a drink. If ever there was a situation calling for desperate remedies this was it, but how would alcohol affect him? He had no experience of the stuff.

Occasionally through the crowd he got a glimpse of Sheila and her bridesmaids, who were got up in garish organdie as if they were deliberately designed to serve as visual foils for the bride. Trust Maura.

Sitting at the top table to eat, he felt like Christ at the last supper, a sacrificial victim hounded into this Gethsemane, ill-used and betrayed, yet still in thrall to his own will. He covered his glass when the wine waiter offered the bottle.

"Padre." He'd have to settle for 'Padre'. Then the second paragraph about Mark: *We knew after the first date … that this was it. No. After the first date. No. Almost after the first date … a fine young man…"*

He pushed his plate away. Chicken and ham and some sort of veg.

"Not hungry?" the groom's mother asked from under her discus hat.

"Not really." Closer it came, with unperturbed majesty, deliberate haste. Hounded now into a corner with no way out.

Then she delivered the fatal thrust, "I'm looking forward to your speech. The Irish are so witty." He recoiled from the touch of her hand on his arm. His temples throbbed with the onset of migraine.

The best man finished reading the telegrams and then Mark was on his feet, smooth and relaxed, weaned on public-school debates, his voice languid and assured. And that accent, those unmatchable vowel sounds: "... and you know when Sheila accepted my proposal I was jolly well bowled over... Her Irish charm ... that certain *je ne sais quoi*..." He held the guests rapt; they murmured approval, and doting smiles appeared on the faces of the womenfolk.

Brendan knew he was next. The weeks of worry he'd already put in didn't ease this moment but instead accumulated into a compound of panicky fear. He'd paid his dues but the account was still due. He groped in his inside pocket for the notes, which were crumpled and sweat-stained. He was next. Any second now. He desperately wanted Mark to finish. He also wanted him to go on and on. Nothing made sense. His mind raced. *Reverend gentlemen ... Mark... When Sheila... Padre...* The words were slipping away from him. Aphasia setting in, his vision blurred. He couldn't do it. He had to. Nothing was worth this.

Suddenly he reached for the nearest wine bottle, filled his glass and gulped it down. The awful unaccustomed taste didn't matter. He had another glass, down in one. He didn't care if anyone noticed. To hell with them all for putting him through this. He was as good as they were, even the Brits. Better maybe, because he could feel. Mark still going on, enjoying himself, the sound of his own voice. Sheila whispering to the best man.

Brendan saw himself struggling to his feet, stumbling forward, lights going dim, words in his throat tumbling out in rag order.

"Break the old pledge, Brendan. Good man. You're entitled." Not unkind. Thank God for hecklers. They might all be sozzled. Think I am too. Good. That gives permission. Friends, this is a perfect day... Yes, he was ready now, thanks to the wine. As ready as he would ever be. Mark finally sitting down to loud applause. No contest. From the corner of his eye he could see the best man rising to his feet to introduce him. Do it quickly while this dispensation lasts. I'm OK ... I'm ready ... looking forward... But what is he saying?

"... Sheila has just told me they have to be at the airport at seven sharp. And the traffic situation is awful. I'm afraid we all went on too long. So, unfortunately we won't be able to call on the father of the bride..."

But I'm ready now, you bastard... To his amazement, Brendan watched the crowd begin to disperse. He jumped up and declaimed loudly to departing backs, "Have a good ... time ... everybody." He stood trembling with relief, but knew that it would soon give way to disgust.

THE EMISSARY GOAT

THE OBJECTIVE OF THE WILD-COW-MILKING event was to see which of six teams of cowboys would be the first to get a half-pint of milk from the untamed prairie cow which had been assigned to each team. Drinking Michelob in the stands surrounding the rodeo ring, we plunked down our bets. At a given signal the four-man teams ran out to their designated cow. Three men tried to hold her while the fourth tried to aim a reluctant teat into the container.

It would have been better fun if not for the fact that one cow was so roughly manhandled that she suffered a broken leg, was shot right there in the arena, the carcase dragged off by a tractor, leaving a large, blood-streaked track in the clay.

This was the Mid-West, the heartland, to which we diplomats had been dispatched from the steaming asphalt and air-conditioned offices of Washington D.C. to spend some days with real Americans (ranchers) on their large, though barely viable, spreads.

My hosts were the Hoddings, a handsome, hard-working couple. Jim Hodding seemed a little ill at ease being part of the scheme – jokingly termed a 'UN Summit' by his fellow ranchers – and probably went along with it for the sake of his wife, Beth, who was very much her own woman, not at all the dimity gingham type of Western folklore. She had already explained to me why she joined the scheme: meeting foreigners was her window on the world. This seemed strange to me because I wouldn't have regarded Montana as parochial exactly. I also wondered if, with me, she hadn't drawn the short straw on this occasion because I didn't regard myself as particularly exotic; in fact there was nowhere in America, no State or city, that made me feel 'foreign' as such.

"I'm sorry you had to see that," Beth said on the way back from the rodeo in the Ford pickup. We were driving through the Amish district just south of Billing.

"Well, it sometimes happens," Jim said.

He pointed to a plump, striated creature caught in the truck's headlights, and steered around the creature who continued his way across the road.

After supper, one of the Hoddings' teenage sons, Thomas, showed me his collection of Indian arrowheads, most of which he'd found on the ranch. They were mainly made of flint and he explained how they had been fixed to the shafts of the arrows. Blackfeet Indians had passed the knowledge on to him. The arrows weren't very effective except for hunting small animals.

The Plains Indians in fact killed most of the buffalo by stampeding them off cliffs and mesas. Beth listened to her son as if for the first time, her facial expressions matching his at every turn. After a final cup of coffee we decided to turn in.

Early the next morning something woke me, some stirring, maybe a door closing. It seemed human in origin – don't ask me how I knew. I waited for another sound to confirm or explain the first. None came. Not until the reassuring clatter of breakfast being prepared some three hours later.

We went to a barbecue that evening on a neighbour's ranch, sat in the long grass under the big sky and compared notes on agriculture. There was a slight language problem: bullock meant steer; they had no word for springer, but we were on common ground with silage and fodder.

At one point, a stork flew overhead on a fairly low flight path.

"Don't stop at my house," Jim called out. "Keep going." He waved his wide-brimmed hat at the large bird, shooing it off into the gathering dusk.

In the days following I learnt a lot about the Hodding ranch, the crops and livestock horses – Jim's pride and joy – which did perform a useful function at round-ups though were kept partly for symbolic reasons. The mystery of the early morning sounds, however, remained and I was loth to inquire about them.

On the last afternoon, when Jim was tending to his horses Beth drove me to 'the west thirty', a huge meadow full of wildflowers where Thomas collected most of his arrowheads. To the north the white peaks of Glacier Park were just about visible while to the east the skyline was serrated by the foothills of the Rockies. It was, by any standard, a breathtaking place, and I knew even before Beth told me that it meant something special to her. We got out of the truck and walked for a while. She told me about her dream – a hopelessly fanciful one – of building a convention centre on that land where people of goodwill could come together.

"A sort of UN?" I inquired.

"No, not exactly … more a … place where people can be themselves… Oh, it's hard to explain." Her smile didn't quite conceal the embarrassment she felt, and I didn't press.

"It's easy to breathe here," I said.

"Yes." She nodded slowly. "Yes it is."

Jim went to bed at eleven that night because he had to be up early the next morning to go to a cattle auction. Beth and I drank coffee in the lounge and talked.

The conversation started slowly, then deepened with the night. She began by saying that a man's priorities in that part of the country were horses, land, boots and belt-buckles in that order; wives came fifth. Although there was humour in her voice, I felt a little uneasy, especially as Jim's muffled snores could be heard through the ceiling.

I didn't have to worry, however, because the next topic she introduced – as if everything that had gone before was merely a prelude – was religion.

She was well versed in comparative religion

and, though formally a Catholic, was keenly interested in the ecumenical movement. For the past two years or so she had organised prayer meetings once a week in the house. They were attended mainly by wives but several different denominations were represented: Baptists, Pentecostalists, Mormons, Amish – and occasionally a woman or two from the Blackfoot reservation would turn up.

"I think I know what kind of convention centre you have in mind. It's a great idea." I said.

"You really think so?" She leant forward, hands clasped between her knees.

"Yes, of course." Her dream was to bring people of good will to that beautiful field and help them develop their spiritual lives regardless of creed or doctrine.

"But you're an Irish Catholic?" The question lingered on her narrow features.

"Well ... yes."

Then she told me that her Parish Priest, Father Mahon, was Irish, that he had asked her to desist from her wrong-headed endeavours, and finally requested that she leave the parish. She was still shocked and saddened by it.

"What age is this Father Mahon?" I inquired.

"About mid-sixties ... why?"

I did a quick calculation. "He would have been brought up in the forties in Ireland and trained for the priesthood in the fifties. They were strange, almost Stalinist, times." She listened intently as I tried to describe the insularity and paranoia of those years, how anyone who showed initiative, especially in spiritual matters, was regarded as a maverick and probably condemned from the pulpit. "Father Mahon is just a product of that system. He probably means well but just can't escape that sort of conditioning. If a priest expelled someone from a parish in Ireland today he'd be laughed at.

"You mean it?"

"Absolutely." I found it hard to grasp the idea of this religious throwback trying to save souls in the Mid-West of America by denying the right of free will. American Catholics weren't exactly progressive, I knew, partly because they were a minority, an enclave, and so developed a fortress outlook, but this was crazy. Time had clearly stood still for this priest, who probably had no idea of the deep hurt he'd caused Beth.

"What you said … it kind of eases my mind. I think…" Beth got up to close a window which let in a sudden draught of night air from the great outdoors. I felt the chill linger in the room. "I think," she continued, "that you've been sent."

It was clear enough that she was being serious and I began to fear that what had started out as a modest conversation might become a bit rich for my blood. While searching for a way to disengage without giving offence – I am a diplomat after all – a thought occurred.

"You get up at five every morning, don't you?" I remembered those unidentifiable noises I had heard.

"Yes."

"To pray?"

"Well, to reflect."

"I thought there were ghosts."

"Only one," Beth said. "A spirit. Or breath."
She smiled.

I had an aisle seat on the flight back to Washington and, during the take-off, buried myself in the in-flight magazine. Tired after my late night conversation with Beth, I nodded off for a while – after we were safely up – and was woken by the stewardess leaning over me to serve a whiskey to the man on my right. I asked for a Bloody Mary and stirred it sleepily with the swizzle stick. I didn't realise that my neighbour was speaking to me; he may have had to repeat himself.

"Judging by the accent, I'd say you're from the Emerald Isle. Would I be correct in that assumption?"

"Yes, quite correct."

"Good man. What are you doing out here?"

It wasn't until I was about half-way through the explanation of the diplomat / heartland stuff – which sounded twee when put into words – that I noticed the Roman collar.

I became instantly alert. It couldn't be … or

could it…?

He kept up a barrage of questions, apparently oblivious of the rudeness of such an unrelenting interrogation. I had the eerie feeling of being located in the cross hairs of a telescopic sight.

"So you stayed on a ranch. Which one?"

"The Hoddings."

"Ah, the Hoddings. Jim's a fine, hard-working man. Wouldn't you say?"

"Yes." Wait, I told myself. Just wait, let it unfold. Don't impede the flow which had taken on a life of its own. I sipped my drink. Just as well I hadn't ordered a Virgin Mary.

"And Missus…?" (Right on cue, without any prompting) "What did you make of that lady?" He twisted his bulky frame, causing me to lean out into the aisle.

"Beth?" This was it, my turn to enter the stream, create eddies, maybe even change the course. "You know, it's funny you should ask that."

"It is?" He stared at me over the rim of his whiskey glass. Had I gone too far too soon?

"Well, you know the sort of upbringing we got in Ireland…" ('We' was a nice touch; it made him smile.) "I mean, I went to the Christian Brothers. I was an altar boy, did the first nine Fridays several times, went to benediction and all the missions…"

"Now you're talking," he said. "Formation," he added, "I had that in St. Peter's Seminary in Wexford. That's what it's all about." His smile became wistful for the days of certainty.

"But do you know what I'm going to tell you? Despite all that formation, as you call it, Beth Hodding taught me more about the real meaning of religion in a few days than I learned in a lifetime. I have never met such a deeply spiritual person."

His eyes slid away and his expression held its own counsel. I didn't look at him again, just nodded slowly to myself in confirmation. A little later his liver-spotted hand moved up to the instrument panel overhead and tinkered with the air conditioning.

I felt a sudden draught of cold air on my face and then, I think, he must have shut off the vent. He didn't say much more during the remainder of the flight, and then it was about Wexford's chances in the League.

Was that the end of the story? No. About a year later I got a letter from Billing, Montana. Eagerly I opened it, hoping to learn that Beth had been welcomed back to the parish. The letter, which was indeed from Beth, made no mention of that at all. Instead, it referred to an enclosed newspaper cutting which reported a hit-and-run accident which had taken the life of Thomas Hodding, oldest son of Jim and Beth Hodding. A small, flint arrowhead slipped out of the envelope into my hand.

ARTIFICIAL INTELLIGENCE

IT WAS A SPRUNG WOOD CHAIR, probably ash, well upholstered, designed for sitting into, rather than perching on. It was snug around Selina's hips and shoulders; she wanted to sleep. But Marilyn, who sat across from her on a slightly higher chair, would not tolerate that.

"Any more thoughts since the last session?" Marilyn asked in her honeysuckle therapist's voice.

"Not really ... still, the guilt ... and regret..." As far as Selina knew, Marilyn had never lost a client. So how could she understand the trauma, the collateral damage, above all, the self-doubt?

"You may still be in shock," Marilyn went on. "But, remember, the guilt feelings will pass. You weren't to know he was suicidal."

"But isn't that our job?" Selina saw it as complete failure, like a bridge collapsing or a plane falling out of the sky. It was the therapist's job to prevent the ultimate act of mental derangement. If it wasn't that then what was it?

"What do you think?" Marilyn batted it back.

"I'd seen him five times, five full sessions." OK, he hadn't ticked all the depression boxes, she thought, but he'd explained how hard his daughter's death had hit him, how it had estranged him from his wife. So, he had tried to deal with it alone like most men, this man called Jack. At the third session he'd said something about action, about how he wasn't much of a thinker but was more into decision-making leading to action. He had been a sportsman; she remembered him from her college days, rowing in the number one boat, though she hadn't ever spoken to him back then.

At their fifth, and what was to be their last, session he said he regarded most situations in life as simple rather than complex. As an engineer he made and fixed things. He had hinted at his frustration; there was nothing he could do to bring his daughter back. How had Selina missed hearing these alarm bells? She had even taken notes. Maybe she just couldn't understand how such a strong man could be so broken. Maybe she'd lost her objectivity and didn't want to believe he was suicidal.

"How do you feel right now?"

"Miserable. Jack … he was a strong person, a good person." A world of Jacks would be a fine place.

"I get the impression he meant more to you than the average client. Might there have been a degree of countertransference…?"

It was true. Selina couldn't help liking him. He was awkward with her, didn't like talking about his feelings. She almost had to seduce him, lead him on in a way that another man could not have done. So, of course there had been a sexual, or rather, gender element to their exchanges. He had laughed just once during the sessions, a deep-throated bark with a slight croak to it. A most welcome sound she would never hear again. He hadn't cried, not even once. She knew he regarded tears as an indulgence; he seemed to prefer the harder route. Certainly, he was the kind of man she could have fallen for, a strong, straight-up guy without a devious bone in his body. His strength of character meant that he didn't need guile in his armoury.

"I liked him." She wondered what Marilyn would make of that? She was more into the techniques of therapy than Selina, who tended to rely on intuition, or 'feel and flair' as the detractors called it.

A feminist had once written that men were in love with death. Selina didn't believe that, though men like Jack had absolutely no fear of death, maybe the manner of dying, especially if it was demeaning and long-drawn-out, but not the fact itself. Despite all her training and all social conventions she could not deny the courage that lay at the heart of self-destruction, the split-second decision that transcended all others, to end the gift of life, of human awareness. It was a strange gift anyway, one that came wrapped in the certain knowledge that it would be taken back. What kind of gift was that? Maybe the feminists had a point; women could cry and talk whereas a man just slung a leather belt over a beam and kicked a chair from under his feet. It was a common practice among the males of all civilisations throughout history. Like referees, they chose when to call full-time, instead of waiting around with heads bowed, knowing the game was lost.

Marilyn loomed over her saying all the right things; it was like waking up to the sound of pigeons cooing in the rafters. Was she afraid Selina, her client now, might top herself? Marilyn had never buried any of her mistakes. In a way this conferred considerable power on Selina. Was suicide ultimately about power – in the same way that rape was?

"Your self-esteem has suffered a terrible blow…"

"A good man is dead," Selina interrupted.

"Yes. He's gone and it is tragic. But you're here." The living had rights, even the unborn, but the dead had none, not even the right to respect or a good name. That was part of Jack's courage; he didn't care about his reputation. Marilyn's covert glance towards the strategically placed clock indicated that the fifty-five minutes were nearly up. She recommended the AIT programme – much to her client's chagrin.

Later that night, after she'd eaten some reheated ravioli, Selina switched on her computer and clicked on the AIT icon, feeling a little foolish. She was a fully trained therapist after all. When she'd unburdened herself, the electronic voice – a mid-Atlantic contralto, accompanied by swooshing tidal sounds, ebbing and flowing, with the occasional wave expiring gently on the beach – urged her not to be so hard on herself.

Selina spoke about the need to be accountable, to accept responsibility. She spoke for a long time, and with more feeling than she could have mustered with Marilyn sitting across from her.

"But you are a good person, a well-meaning person," the contralto replied at length.

Selina took issue with that and spoke about mixed motives and subtexts. When she had finished the response came, "That is all part of our humanity. We are not gods but people. Sometimes, unfortunately our best efforts are not good enough. But if we do our best we can do no more."

To her consternation Selina felt tears well up in her eyes and then she wept loudly for a while.

"Let it all out," the voice continued. The sound of a nose being blown led to the exhortation being repeated.

She endured AIT for another ten minutes, not sure whether she or the machine was following the script. She switched off the computer and it went dead with a brief wheeze. The programmed mantra of praise and reassurance had done her some good even though she saw through it, but the modest benefit wasn't going to last long.

Jack had said something else about modern life – too much freedom and not enough guidelines, resulting in too few values. He had put it more or less like that, almost a mathematical equation. After his daughter's death and the breakdown of his marriage there was no lodestar for him to steer by. Everything he valued had been taken from him. It wasn't self-pity, and removing himself from the scene was the simple logic of not having anything to live for. It wasn't a *felon de se* but a vindicated brave and logical act. Now that it was all so clear to her in retrospect – the way he reasoned and decided – she felt even more stupid and ashamed for having missed it during their sessions.

Psychology was a soft science, of course. There were no firm laws of behaviour. It was nondirective, nonjudgmental, maybe nonlogical, nowadays more behavioural than Freudian but she knew the evidence which was a closely guarded secret: there was no empirical support whatsoever that psychotherapy had ever helped anybody. Psychiatry wasn't much better; it was the only branch of medicine that had no basis in science or research into the functioning of the brain. Most clients who improved would probably have improved anyway even if they'd been living on a desert island. If you got the client to cry, it was a major selling point because tears released endorphins in the brain and made the client feel good. Chemistry was where it was at. What kind of snake oil were she and Marilyn peddling? They liked to see themselves as professionals; that simply meant they got paid. Better by far if they were amateurs and did it for love.

Some years ago she used to watch The Sopranos on TV. If the Mafia ever found out that their Capo was spilling his guts to a shrink he would be killed immediately – and so would the shrink. The fear of sleeping with the fishes lent a frisson to their exchanges, although it was never clear whether the shrink fully realised the danger she was in. Was the Mafia's disdain of her profession wrong?

There should be sanctions. Lose a client, spend some time in jail. At least show remorse.

Jack hadn't agonised over issues multifaceted or otherwise; there was no Hamlet-style dithering and moodiness. He just went and killed himself.

She tried to watch TV but found herself surfing from one channel to another unable to commit to any. She began to lose contact with the ground under her feet and, like the mythical Antaeus, felt vulnerable without any purchase on the earth. By midnight she had reached a limit. She had approached it slowly and imperceptibly but with deadly fidelity as if it had been planned in some part of her brain for a long time.

She lay in bed feeling the effects of the pills and booze. She was floating, still above the ground but it didn't matter anymore; it was not unpleasant. Chemistry was the answer. However, as she began to nod off, some resistance grew inside her. It was similar to the desire to fight off sleep when driving a car. She could have a few more reasonable years on the planet, ameliorated by prescription drugs if necessary. Dying now would be a mistake. She didn't have Jack's single-minded determination. She fumbled for her cell phone and managed to call the emergency number before she passed out.

She had little recollection of A and E or of having her stomach pumped. When she came to some twenty hours later, Marilyn was standing over the bed, a concerned look on her face.

"Thank goodness you're all right."

"I'm alive … not quite the same thing…"

"What have you done?"

"Nothing … that's the problem." She had failed … not like Jack. Her effort was a measly, pathetic cry for help. Still, she had flexed her muscles and was a minor stain on Marilyn's escutcheon. Would it cause Marilyn to question her profession, analyse the snake oil? – probably not. That one-time laugh of Jack's was like a sudden wave breaking at the back of his throat, a dry, sympathetic laugh. She thought she could hear it now, echoing faintly through the corridors.

DRIVEN TO EXCESS

WHAT WALTER SUGRUE SAW on his desk that day after lunch shocked him so badly that he jumped backwards and broke the glass of a framed print with the back of his head. He was unaware of the small trickle of blood that crept through his sparse grey hairs until it reached the back of his neck. Then he began to shake, though mainly with anger…

Some three and a half years earlier Tommy Hanrahan had been assigned to him as an Executive Assistant in Personnel. Walter's previous assistant had gone on to greater things and he felt as if he were being used to break in another young colt. He was hard on Tommy from the very beginning, especially when he learnt that he had successfully completed a night degree in French and German. The Vice Secretary General of the Department had made it clear in an internal memo that languages were at a premium, because of EU membership.

In Sugrue's eyes Tommy, who was at least twenty years younger, was in the fast track and could well overtake him, which, in the feverish parlance of the Department, was a fate worse than death. He buried Tommy in menial tasks, making him spend most of his time in the dusty registry going through old files looking up precedents. His knowledge of German and French wouldn't do him any good in that crypt of rotting paper, without a computer in sight.

The high point of Tommy's first year involved a compensation case in which a lady clerk sought recompense for laddering her tights on a metal in-tray. After two pages of well-reasoned argument, Tommy concluded that, on balance, compensation was in order, less 10 percent for depreciation of said tights. Walter Sugrue disagreed and in *his* memo argued that the in-tray had been in its usual position, that the claimant had passed by it several times a day for twelve years without mishap. There was a coy suggestion that the Department could hardly be held accountable for the introduction of the miniskirt ("the vagaries of ladies' fashions"). There was also a suggestion that Mr. Thomas Hanrahan was rather free and easy with the Department's money.

Tommy was taken aback by this rebuttal and when he asked Walter Sugrue where exactly his argument was flawed, he got a curt response.

"You were in error."

He felt like a heretic.

The next case Tommy dealt with – revised leave allowance for one of the blue-collar grades – also went sour on him. He made comparisons with similar grades outside the Department and again "erred" on the side of generosity.

"Outside comparisons are irrelevant," Sugrue said. "Internal relativities are all that matter." He sat bolt upright at his desk, hardly looking at Tommy whose desk was further away from the window. "We don't concern ourselves with what goes on out there." He waved dismissively in the direction of the window.

"But surely it's a competitive market…"

"Do you realise what would have happened if I had not reversed your … am … recommendation? The internal auditor would have had a field day. And the Vice Secretary General could have been severely embarrassed. What if the matter became *public*?"

"Oh I doubt if…"

"I can assure you there is no doubt about it. I'm dismayed by your attitude. You don't seem to realise the enormity of what could have happened. Now, please go back to work." Sugrue picked up his Parker fountain pen and began scratching with it. When he had finished writing he punched a hole in the corner of the paper with a sort of pliers and affixed it to the file by means of a Treasury tag. He addressed the file to the Vice Secretary General and placed it in the out-tray. He regarded the new-fangled personal computer as a fad and one which could not be trusted. He had heard that something called hard drives could not be deleted and could, therefore, return to haunt the user. There was also the possibility of being approached by women of easy virtue in places known as 'chat rooms'.

From beneath furrowed brows, Tommy watched all these delicate and fastidious movements, during which Sugrue's expression never changed, apart from the occasional wetting of lips by a lizard-like tongue. He knew now what he had long suspected – he would get no quarter from Walter Sugrue. The man hated him, not with passion but with a coldness that chilled him to the bone.

He was right. At the end of the first year an increment was withheld – based on a secret recommendation from Sugrue. Tommy could only surmise where he had gone wrong. OK, he was inclined to err on the liberal side; that was clearly not consistent with the 'culture' of the Department. Also he had tried to develop a new way of assessing relativity claims. That had blown up in his face. He would not try to be 'creative' again. Better to keep his head down and go by the book.

His next compensation case involved an Irish embassy abroad. There had been a party which had clearly gotten out of hand because the building had gone on fire. The ambassador had lodged a claim on behalf of himself and his wife. Since the State insured its own embassies abroad, the amount claimed would have to be paid by the taxpayer. Tommy set to with a will, deleting many items of furniture, paintings and personal bric-à-brac, and discounting heavily the designer dresses of the ambassador's wife. After his diligence he found that he had knocked almost two thirds off the claim – surely a good day's work. Walter Sugrue was horrified and wondered if Tommy knew anything about his job.

Tommy was genuinely shocked. "I reduced

the claim to about one third," he said. "It was inflated, padded out. Isn't it our job to save money on behalf of the taxpayer?"

"There shouldn't have been any reduction," Sugrue said. "Don't you understand anything. The ambassador is one of us…"

Tommy decided to keep his head down even further. It was easier than he'd expected. After a while it became second nature. Less was more; the minimalist's credo. All of his colleagues practised the art. Nevertheless, Tommy couldn't quite forgive Sugrue for making him a cynical old bastard before his time. This went harder with him than losing an increment, which in a way gave him a certain cachet in the Department, especially with colleagues of his own grade to whom, at a tea break, he had uttered the line: "I regard it not so much as losing an increment as gaining an excrement".

Shortly after that, Sugrue had to get a briefing note to the Vice Secretary General as a matter of urgency. He sent Tommy upstairs with it. Walking down the corridor quickly (it didn't do to be seen strolling or loitering in the public passageways), he saw the Vice Secretary General leave his office and walk towards the stairs. Tommy knew he wanted the brief for the business lunch he was rushing to attend. He might have had time to catch him up in the corridor. But he decided not to bother. Running was not part of his job description. He handed the brief to the Personal Assistant.

That afternoon Sugrue got a memo from above, saying how dismayed the Vice Secretary General was that the briefing had not been ready on time. 'Dismay' was the most frequently felt emotion in the Department – perhaps the only one. Everyone was dismayed regularly, at least three or four times a week.

Ashen-faced, Sugrue turned on Tommy, "It was before 1 p.m. when you went up with the brief."

"Possibly. I gave it immediately to his Personal Assistant."

"Why didn't he get it then?"

Tommy was going to suggest that the PA may have been slow off the mark, but decided against it. "Maybe he'd already gone out to lunch."

"Didn't you ask?" Sugrue removed his wire glasses with a slow wide sweep of his arm.

"I assumed he was still in his office." Tommy noticed how Sugrue's lower lip disappeared under his yellowing buck teeth. This was a moment he would savour. Sticking rigidly to his brief, and using no initiative, gave him complete protection. Or so he thought.

On the following Friday, Walter Sugrue announced that an important letter was missing from a file.

"I remember it," Tommy said. "It was on the file when I was dealing with it."

"Well, it's not there now. Please institute a search immediately."

Tommy did so, visiting all of the offices the file had travelled through in the past month, but the letter didn't turn up. A second search fared no better and Tommy had to take the rap. He became convinced that Sugrue had deliberately removed the latter from the file to get him into trouble. Mainly because of that ('poor administrative practice') another increment was withheld on the due date. Sugrue was doing him in and there was no court of appeal, not in a hierarchy. The atmosphere in the office became poisonous. People who dropped in from time to time could sense the mood; it was as if invisible venom issued from the faintly scratching pens. It was not a happy scriptorium.

Sometimes when Tommy's mind wandered and he found himself gazing out the window at the tops of double-decker buses passing by, he would hear the reprimanding throat-clearings of Sugrue which brought him back to reality – a reality which was not too demanding but one which offered no excitement or sense of achievement. Sugrue, however, seemed to relish small triumphs, especially at the expense of others. In a way this frightened Tommy, because the day might come when he too would settle for a life like that. It was indeed a scary prospect.

The breaking point came when the Vice Secretary General sent a note to Sugrue about the eligibility criteria for promotion. He suggested that some weight should be given to academic qualifications. Sugrue was not seized of the idea;

in fact it was clear that he would do everything in his power to strangle the idea at birth.

"We'll be hiring professors next," he muttered. All of the experienced officers like himself, who had laboured in the salt mines for years, would be passed over by lazy boffins. His written response was far more muted of course. He wrote that "the notion would be considered in detail." This was a stalling tactic employed in the hope that the loathsome idea would simply wither on the vine in the fullness of time.

Later that afternoon a porter came to empty the out-trays. Tommy followed him outside.

"Just a second, Barney, I want to have another look at that memo." Taking a propelling pencil from his top pocket, Tommy neatly inserted inverted commas around the word 'notion'.

The subsequent row was even more heated than he anticipated. The first thing to happen was that Sugrue received a memo from the Vice Secretary General which took him to task:

"Mr. Sugrue,

If you do not agree with my 'notions' why not just say so…?"

The Vice Secretary General had added an 's' to the offending word, thereby adding insult to injury.

"Christ, what's got him so riled up?" Sugrue asked aloud. "I didn't debunk his idea, even if it is nonsense." He was genuinely scared. He scratched his head which, though bald, produced a small flurry of dandruff.

"Maybe the office is bugged." Tommy said as a joke, but Sugrue threw him a contemptuous look. His rodent rose quivered.

Eventually Sugrue saw the original memo – which Tommy failed to intercept – and he immediately noticed the inverted commas.

"Who put those in?" he yelled as if in pain.

"What?" Tommy asked. He had taken a risk and now it looked like backfiring.

Sugrue pointed with a trembling finger, "I didn't put those in. So who did?"

"Beats me."

Sugrue went through various possibilities in his head then turned to Tommy.

"You did it. Didn't up?"

"Absolutely not. And I have to say I am dismayed to hear such…"

But Sugrue knew. He knew all right. Tommy would have to be very careful.

A few weeks later, when Tommy was in the Registry, he had an opportunity to slip unnoticed into the Personnel section, which was normally off limits. He had a peek at his own personal file and was astounded to find several notes and memos on it from Sugrue expressing dismay at the quality of his work. The most vitriolic one was dated the day after the inverted commas incident. According to Sugrue, he had been driven to the conclusion that Mr Thomas

Hanrahan had sabotaged a memorandum prepared by a senior officer, a devious act which had caused the Vice Secretary General considerable dismay.

Tommy dashed off his own memo:

"To: Mr. Walter Sugrue

From: Mr. Thomas Hanrahan, 10 March

I recently happened to some across my personal file and noticed therein several memos from you criticising my work. I was dismayed by this chance discovery, especially as you have not spoken to me about any of these matters and have rushed to conclusions without any semblance of due process. Perhaps you could explain why you went behind my back…?"

He sat and watched Sugrue as he opened the envelope and read the memo.

Sugrue coloured slightly, coughed, reached for a pen, and began scratching.

The next day Tommy received the following memo, which a rather irate porter took from Sugrue's out-tray and transferred to Tommy's in-tray – a distance of ten feet – rolling his eyes to heaven as he did so.

"To: Mr. Thomas Hanrahan

From: Mr. Walter Sugrue, 11 March

Re: Your memo of 10 March last, it surely must come as no surprise to you that I consider your work to be substandard and shoddy. You have already been docked two increments – virtually unprecedented in this Department. As to the nature of your deficiencies, I should have thought these were obvious, even to you. Nevertheless, I will remind you of the egregious errors you made some time ago in relation to compensation cases and leave allowances for porters.

Finally, I have to say how dismayed I am that you have breached the regulations of the Department by consulting your own personal file. This is intolerable. I will have to discuss these and other matters with the Vice Secretary General…"

Tommy debated long and hard with himself. In a way he knew he couldn't win. Hierarchies were designed that way. He knew that Sugrue had not forgotten the inverted commas and was out to get him.

He eventually decided on the following:

"To: Mr. Walter Sugrue
From: Mr. Thomas Hanrahan 15 March
It is obvious from the tone of your memo of 11 march last that there is a serious personality clash in this office which has become intolerable. I have tried my best to ameliorate the situation and am dismayed by the fact that matters are getting worse. In the circumstances, I must request a transfer to another Section as a matter of urgency…"

For some reason he couldn't resist adding the flourish, "I do not envy my replacement in this office." He made it clear that he had copied the memo to the Vice Secretary General.

That final barb made Sugrue jump in his chair. He fixed his specs, which had become dislodged in the jump, and began to write. The final draft which Tommy received some days later was as follows:

"To: Mr. Thomas Hanrahan

From: Mr. Walter Sugrue 20 March

Re your extraordinary memo of 15 March last I have had discussions with the Vice Secretary General to whom, I note, you copied your memo of 15 march last, thereby going over my head.

It has been agreed that you should indeed be transferred since you are obviously not capable of doing your present job. It has been decided to transfer you to the Registry where you should report to Miss Hanlon at 9 a.m. next Monday. She will explain your duties to you. Since they will be mainly of a manual and repetitive nature, you should be able to undertake them with some degree of efficiency.

This transfer does of course imply a demotion of two grades, and a substantial decrease in salary and pension rights. I am dismayed that your behaviour has left us with no alternative. If you do not perform your new duties to the standard expected, you will be dismissed.

Let me have your response soonest..."

Disbelief turned to anger as Tommy reread the turgid prose – a hate poem. He knew he couldn't win. But to be shafted by such a little shit as Sugrue, hiding behind the bureaucracy, was too much, too much to bear. And that was why, to everyone's astonishment when the news got out, he brought the memo with him to the W.C. and later left it, in a rather altered state, on Sugrue's desk before he came back from lunch.

DRIVEN MAD

BILLY LOOKED AT HIS DIARY and felt disappointed. It was over two years since he had sent his manuscript off to Shuttle and Brood to be considered, and in all of that time he heard nothing, not even an acknowledgement of its receipt. He sent off a letter to the Editor of S and B, a lady called Millicent Aspartame:

"Dear Ms Aspartame,
I sent you the full manuscript of my novel, Ebb Tide, on the 17th of February 2013. I wonder if you are yet in a position to decide on this submission? It has been over two years after all.
Yours sincerely
Billy MacAleese "

Six months later to the day Billy got the following reply:

"Dear Mr. MacAleese,
We have read your novel, Ebb Tidal, and while we liked it in parts, have concluded that it is not suitable for our list.
It seemed to our reader that the main character, Adrian, should not have gambled while on vacation in Nice, especially as his business was in trouble.
Thank you for thinking of Shuttle and Brood.

Yours sincerely,
Anne Green for Ms Aspartame."

Billy spent a lot of time on that letter and on the tangled question of whether he should reply or not. Could they not have told him which parts they liked? Why did they get the title wrong, and why had Ms Aspartame not signed it herself – surely she owed him that much after a two-year delay? And of course they got Adrian's character wrong. Yes, he took a risk in the casinos of Nice but, as an entrepreneur, he was not afraid of risk – which he had to confront every day of his life, managing the glass factory. These people in Shuttle and Brood clearly had no conception of real entrepreneurship or indeed of life itself. He couldn't really let them away with it.

He sent them a polite response, setting out his four points of departure. He expected that that would be the end of the matter but to his surprise he received a reply and, what was even more extraordinary was that it came almost by return post.

"Dear Mr MacAleese,
Re your letter of 17 last, we do not normally reply to missives of this sort. However, there was an inference in your letter to the effect that, because of a typo, we treated your work cavalierly. This is not so. Once your manuscript, an unsolicited one, came to the surface of the so-called slush pile, it was read with due care and

diligence.

To repeat, the main character, Adrian, did not ring true, and moreover, your novel does not fall into any of the genres we specified.

Incidentally, we have now changed our policy and no longer accept unagented manuscripts.

Yours etc.

Millicent Aspartame"

Billy brought the letter to the pub with him. He sat in a corner under the clock and read it twice per pint. At least Millicent Aspartame had signed it this time, but that was cold comfort. After four pints he drew a biro from an inside pocket and began to make notes on his newspaper for a reply. The beer helped his imagination but the wording left a lot to be desired and over the next two days he edited the draft quite a bit. He wanted the tone to be statesmanlike, unemotional, and he wanted to occupy the high ground, and not muddy his boots by descending into the enteric marketplace. He wrote:

"Dear Ms Aspartame,

I have your letter of 20th last and note that Shuttle and Brood do not any longer accept unagented manuscripts.

I did not wish to suggest that you treated my work cavalierly but rather that your judgment is perhaps lacking in some respects. This may simply reflect your fixation on genre – and no doubt on the bottom line. The truth is that life does not fall into your neat categories or genres which in any case have no meaning in a postmodern and syncretic world.

I can understand how and why categories help your business. You can advertise a genre, compare and contrast with other genres, etc. Categorisation gives you a language of labels and makes your life so much easier. Imagine having to market a book that is part thriller, part romance, part horror, part fantasy, part mainstream. It could cause you angst; no elevator pitch would be possible. Such a hodgepodge of a book would not be recognisable – or marketable – and yet life is like that, is it not? The print media have not recognised this simple fact.

But TV and other media have. *The Wire* revolutionised TV by presenting a show that was based on life as much as it was on Crime. Larry David did much the same with *Seinfeld* and *Curb Your Enthusiasm* by breaking down the walls between Sitcoms and life. It is not a Hobbesian world or even a Cartesian one.

I have re-read some other desiderata of Shuttle and Brood. You want the reader to become engaged in the very first paragraph which should promise some catastrophe. Women in jeopardy attract empathy, according to you. And a dash of Sapphic behaviour can season the mix. Might I point out that we are not making an exploding cake. Readers should not be patronised or treated like idiots.

And you and other publishing houses are the gatekeepers. You are supposed to facilitate good work and keep out the bad. But you do not filter; you do the opposite. You let the sludge through and keep out the pure water. Listen to me: marketability is not the criterion. Quality is. Novels are not widgets to be turned out and sold by the ton. It would be too much to expect you to raise standards but surely you could make some effort to maintain them at least? Or is that too much to ask?

Yours sincerely
Billy MacAleese"

This sparked the following reply which arrived some days later:

"Dear Mr MacAleese,
I have your letter of 24th. I wish to advise you to fuck off.

Yours most sincerely,
Millicant Aspartame"

Billy didn't know whether to be pleased or outraged. He had obviously struck a chord. In a way he had got a result. On the other hand the swear word did cut him to the quick. He had never been told to fuck off before, not even in an email or text message, and only rarely in a blog or tweet. Was it conceivable that the publishing industry was more trammelled in the mire than he had realised? Had tabloidism and text messaging reached epidemic proportions? Popular culture had a lot to answer for.

On the other hand, maybe he had been condescending and snobbish. Were Shuttle and Brood driving standards down or were they simply responding to the revealed preferences of the marketplace? Surely there was more to life and art than pandering and titillation?

He had a desire to write back and tell her to fuck off as well, but his literary sensibilities screamed 'no'. Although he hated it he would have to leave Ms Aspartame with the last word, even though that was what she obviously wanted. But what could he write back? There was no way he could raise himself up out of the pig slop into which she had dragged him. The bonus for him was that he had forced her to reveal her true, dark, nature. But was that enough to right the wrong done to him by Ms Aspartame of Shuttle and Brood?

He decided not to extend the correspondence. Instead he would write a short story about the matter and get it published in a proper literary magazine.

DROWNING CONTINUOUSLY IN BAPTISMAL WATER

SOMETIMES WHEN HE SAW THE CHILD struggling in the water, Patrick could almost convince himself that it was just a bad dream. He would see the child's head being swamped by the river in flood, hands waving frantically as they threshed hopelessly for something to hold. He would see the head go under while the left hand somehow remained aloft, the thin arm sloping backwards as the child was swept downstream by the current. Then everything disappeared except the torrents, and he knew it was not a dream.

From the safety of the bank he had watched his son drown, his only son, Mark, not yet five years old. One second he was above the water, then suddenly below, dragged away, never to re-appear – though his body was discovered later by divers.

Patrick had gone through the funeral in a trance, not really believing it was Mark who lay in the white coffin.

For sixteen years he was haunted, day and night, by the same question. Why had he not dived in to save him? He couldn't swim well but that did not exonerate him. He was Mark's father and he watched his son drown. God in Heaven, nothing could excuse or explain what he had done, or rather failed to do.

It didn't matter that he became a pariah and a recluse. People were right about him; he had no argument with them or with his wife who had left him eight months after the tragedy. It was right that he be abandoned since he had abandoned his son in an unimaginably worse way. He often considered suicide but lacked the guts for that; he settled for self-harming even though the cuts to his arms offered a temporary diversion only.

Maybe because of some survival instinct he would sometimes escape into fantasies about strange and powerful forces that had held him back at the critical moment. On occasion the fantasies were more mundane: his wife had screamed at him not to jump in, a group of men had restrained him.

Once, Mark told him in a dream not to blame himself because he, Patrick, had become catatonic and therefore the question of fear did not arise. On another occasion he dreamt that Mark was alive and working as a teacher. There had been no accident, no dilemma. He'd imagined the whole thing just to test himself. Patrick woke from those dreams refreshed, but the new man who seemed to have taken his place soon faded away and the blackness returned. Facts were brutal; they took no prisoners.

Every day for sixteen years Patrick had tried to remember what went through his mind at the time and for sixteen years he had failed. There was only an amorphous feeling of dread. He didn't know why he had hesitated or what had caused that moment of fatal cowardice. All he knew for certain was that if he had known then what the rest of his life would be like he would have dived in without a second's hesitation. He would have flailed around and drowned along with Mark, both of them going down into the muddy torrents, into the quieter water below, hands and hair floating upwards, lungs filling... Maybe he could have embraced his son before the last moment came.

The nonstop search for justification fed his self-loathing. He should spend more time thinking about Mark's suffering and lonely death and all the years of life that had been taken from him. What might he have done with his life? What might he not have achieved?

Patrick remembered holding Mark in his arms shortly after he was born. The infant changed his life, gave it meaning where there was none before. How had he repaid that gift?

For sixteen years Patrick had visited the riverbank in his mind but had never gone back there. On Mark's twentieth anniversary he plucked up enough courage to do just that.

As he drove out of the city into the country the sun broke through some low cloud cover and for the first time in his life Patrick felt a tinge of redemptive peace; it was real, not just a dream or a product of his imagination. He parked the car in a field and walked towards the river. The ground was soft and yielding after the recent rain; it became marshy as he neared the river. The picnic tables were still there though some of them were in bad condition, split along the grain and soft with wet rot. He recognised the willow which marked the spot. Proximity didn't hurt as much as he had feared.

He reached the bank and noticed the patch of reeds where Mark had fallen in. He gazed at the mud coloured water, and every one of the dreams he'd had of rescuing his son coalesced in his mind. Without fully realising what he was doing, he jumped over the reeds right into the river. Suicide was not far from his thoughts, but he was driven by something else. The water shocked him and began to draw him under. He didn't resist much. It wasn't so bad. What had he been afraid of all those years ago? He opened his eyes under water and saw the light filtering through the sap green depths. This was what Mark had seen. He was joining him at last; it was as if the last sixteen years had melted away. It was possible to put the clock back after all, make amends. He was drowning but he felt cleansed. It was as it should always have been.

But something was wrong. His head broke the surface of the water; sunlight suffused him. His lungs filled automatically with pure air. It took some time for him to realise that he was standing on the riverbed. He shifted from one foot to the other, hoping it might just be a rock or a ledge of some kind. No, it was the riverbed; the water was no more than four feet deep. He waded towards the reeds and lay among them in agony.

ORIENTEERING

THEY WERE STILL WALKING around noon. Sam was pushing his daughter in an ordinary stroller. Belinda was pushing her son in a high-tech stroller which had a shelf for parcels and a hinged hood to protect the infant from sudden showers.

"I don't know why she gave that little cry," Sam said about his daughter. "I changed her nappy about twenty minutes ago, and it can't be wind."

"Oh, she probably senses things," Belinda said. She nodded towards her offspring in the high-tech stroller. "This little fellow is the opposite. There's never a peep out of him."

"Yes, he's placid all right." That's what one said about quiet children. Placid, was the word. Did that mean they didn't sense things? He wasn't sure.

There was a sort of dolmen or standing stone to the left of the hill path they walked on. The stone cast a shadow on the grass. Sam studied it for a while. "It must be nearly one," he said.

"It doesn't matter." Belinda raised one wheel of the stroller to avoid a clump of goats' currents that lay on the path.

"Maybe we should eat our sandwiches."

She shook her head. "There's no need. Let's get on."

They followed the path, which had become

less defined. In fact it was quickly disappearing as a path. The vegetation that grew over it was short-stemmed, of a mosslike quality which did not snag the wheels of the strollers. So they continued even though after a while the path, to all intents and purposes, ran out. It was a path no more.

"What you said back then … 'Let's get on…' That's fine. But where? That's my question." He looked sideways at her and at her son who was trailing his little fingers along the mossy surface.

"That's immaterial." She sighed and breathed in the warm, sweet air. "This is wonderful. 'For we on honeydew have fed, and drunk the mild of paradise.' *Are* feeding, *are* drinking."

"That's all very well…" he began.

"You can say that again."

"What I mean is … what is our destination? Have we got one in mind? Have we a plan?" He bent to pick up a plastic rattle that his daughter had just thrown on the ground. He wagged his finger as he handed it back to her.

Then he noticed that pieces of clay were adhering to the rattle where she had left bits of spit. He rubbed the rattle several times against the leg of his trousers, then took out his handkerchief, gave the rattle a thorough clean and handed it back to her in the nick of time, i.e., before she started to bawl. Her little fat hands, which had been impatiently opening and closing in frustrated grasping efforts, finally comprehended the toy which she immediately shoved in her mouth.

Belinda watched this play as if from a distance. "Did you plan that? No. Just look at the sky. Breathless it is. The clouds spread out like sails but hardly moving. What is their destination? Becalmed. Be calm."

Sam craned his neck and looked up. He felt dizzy for a while and only recovered his balance by returning his eyes to the ground. The bright light of the sky still lingered in his head and made him sneeze. He thought he would never be able to stop; they were powerful sneezes that buckled his thin frame. Spasm succeeded spasm. Belinda smiled indulgently through all the convulsions and, when he finally finished, said, "The case rests."

Her son was looking closely at Sam with an unnervingly frank stare that bored right through him.

"He's probably never seen anyone sneeze before," Sam said, not sure why he felt there was something to justify. His daughter would probably have howled were it not for the rattle that was now firmly ensconced in her mouth. Sam examined it for the umpteenth time, reassuring himself that she couldn't swallow it. And the plastic was colour-fast. So, it was all right.

"Oh, he has seen that," Belinda said. "Many times. It's just that he's curious about everything, even about things that are repeated…"

"That reminds me," Sam interrupted her

without meaning to, "That wood over there looks familiar. It's not a wood really, more … a copse. But I think we've been this way before."

Belinda took her sight line from his pointing finger. "Could be. I can hear a sparrowhawk."

"If I'm right, we should see a river when we get to the top of this hill."

They walked on. It was now well past midday, probably approaching afternoon, if not indeed the beginning of evening. The sun was still very hot, however, and Sam was glad he'd brought a straw hat for his sparsely thatched dome, and a light cotton bonnet for his curly-headed daughter.

When they reached the brow of the hill there was a small valley but no river.

Sam raised his hat and scratched his head. "I'm confused."

"Confusion is just a state of mind," Belinda said.

They began to walk down the gentle slope of the riverless valley. They had to lean back a little so that the strollers wouldn't run away on them.

"That's a tautology." He grinned; it wasn't often he got the upper hand.

"It's a trope," she said but didn't elaborate. She gave him a sudden, darting glance. "I know what you're going to say next."

"What?"

"Not that."

"Then what?"

"Not that either."

He clammed up and concentrated on pushing, or rather steering, the stroller. His mouth was set in a stern line at a right angle to the direction they followed. He seemed determined to get wherever they were going.

"I wonder where we've come from?" he mused aloud.

"That's it!" Belinda clapped her plump hands in triumph.

"What?" He was slow on the uptake.

"I knew that's what you were going to say." She gave him a fullblown smile that revealed most of her fine, cylindrical teeth, some of which caught the sun's rays.

"How do I know you got it right?"

"That doesn't matter. *I* know I got it right. That's all that counts." Belinda leant forward and patted her son's head as if he too had a share in her success.

"Well, what's the answer?"

"I can't be expected to know everything." She looked up and closed her eyes against the sunlight, which bathed her face in a golden glow. There was something almost theatrical about the colour and about her expression as if a powerful spotlight had picked her out. She inhaled slowly and sumptuously through slightly dilated nostrils.

It was amazing how she enjoyed the moment, exulted in it. He had always tried to learn from her but he lacked the serene disposition. But he was prepared to try again, so he also raised his face to the sky and this time he didn't sneeze. He was just on the verge of sharing her experience when the old familiar dizzy sensation took over. Despite the vertiginous flashes, he held his posture but spread his feet wider to maintain balance and tried to strengthen his grip on the push-bar of the stroller. For a split second there was a prospect of succeeding and if he succeeded even once he felt he could transform himself and became more like Belinda. That was the prize being offered, but suddenly he lost his balance.

When he came to he was lying in mud, soaked to the skin. He must have been unconscious for a long time; there hadn't been a dark cloud in the sky the last time he'd looked up. Now, it was all different but he was still lost; there was no river in the valley. Belinda and the children were gone. He got to his knees and began to wipe the mud from his eyes.

FABLED ISLE

YEARS AGO WHEN THE WORLD was more innocent than it is today, there existed an island of wonderful, friendly people who lived in peace and loved their king.

There was a mountain close to the centre of the island and it was rich in gold. The people were not greedy, however, and since the invaders left they only mined as much gold as they needed for food, shelter and other necessities. True to their faith, they did not believe that luxuries, which could easily be imported from the Mainland led to happiness. They also wanted to leave plenty of gold in the mountain for the next generation and the ones after that.

The people were fond of reading and talking. Apart from a little gold-mining, a few of them did some fishing every now and again. One of these was a boy called Vincent, who knew the seas like the back of his hand and could tell by looking at the surface of the water where the shoals of fish were. He loved water and was intrigued by how it was taken up into the clouds and then fed back as rainfall into the rivers and seas. To him it was more precious than gold.

The king had grown old and feeble. When he died there was great mourning and the poets and storytellers set about the task of turning him into a legend. It was soon announced by the courtiers that the young prince, Sadim, would accede to the throne. When the dead king's funeral was over, plans were made to celebrate Prince Sadim's investiture, which took place in the Great Hall of the palace. After all the excitement died down the people went back to their houses to read the poetry and stories which had been written to commemorate the recent events. They liked the new king very much; he was a great storyteller and got on well with his courtiers and advisers. The island would prosper under his reign as it had done under his father's reign.

The fisherboy, Vincent, was happy at his trade. His canoe was old and he had to repair it often. He liked to paddle it from the estuary up the island's one river, which flowed down the gold mountain. Some of the old mines had left large holes in the mountain, which the river filled with water. Vincent liked to swim in these lakes after he had caught enough fish for the day.

On one such day, after he had emerged from the lake and put on his clothes, he walked further up the mountain. When he was about half way from the summit he could see in the distance one of the towers of the palace and the flag flying on top of it. The flag had a blue background, representing the sea, and a yellow triangle, representing the gold mountain.

It might have been this distraction which contributed to the accident. Without any warning the ground gave way under his feet and he fell through a crevasse into a large cavern. When he got his wind back he managed to climb out. He sat on a rock for a long time lost in thought. As he paddled down-river he heard the sound of pile-drivers and noticed that a jetty was being built on one of the largest lakes. According to a large sign, the project was being funded by the Mainland. He continued on his journey and when he got home he decided to build himself a better boat.

Some weeks later, King Sadim celebrated his fortieth birthday. Many people were invited to the palace and, by all accounts, had a wonderful time. They relived the events in the town's square on the following day of rest. Vincent overheard some of the conversation. The Mayor said he had never before tasted food and drink of the quality provided by the new King and, on top of all that, His Majesty had great wit and a clever turn of phrase. They could be proud of him when he went abroad to meet other VIPs. Everyone agreed. Another man said that the new works of art collected by the King would be a great legacy for the people. A woman pointed out how lucky they were that the King was not a spendthrift; he had spent little on the palace which, truth be told, was showing signs of wear and tear. Even though taxes had gone up, they were still quite low because of the gold in the mountain.

Vincent attempted to say something and explain what he had seen, but no one listened to him. The people were so excited by their visit to the palace and by the charm of King Sadim that nothing else seemed to matter. They regarded

Vincent as that strange orphan kid who preferred water to gold.

A little while later Vincent tested his new boat. It had a sail and was a good deal larger than the canoe. Having finished his fishing for the day, he sailed the boat up-river, moored it and went for a swim in his favourite lake. The water was much deeper than before and the lake seemed to have grown wider and longer. When he got back to his boat he shinned up the mast to have a better view. Several of the lakes had burst their banks and merged together. The cavern he had fallen into on his last trip was now filled with water. The river was in flood and its course was reversed; it now fed the lakes rather than the sea. He sampled the water and got the taste of salt. His worst fears were confirmed: the sea was invading because the mountain was sinking.

He noticed trucks driving along the new jetty and come to a stop at the end. Then he saw the Royal Yacht appear. A huge crane unloaded the trucks and filled the hold of the yacht with gold. King Sadim came on deck every now and again to direct operations. Eventually, when the hold was full of gold the King gave the order and the yacht weighed anchor and sailed away, leaving his palace and the island behind in the emerald mist.

By now the lakes were overflowing and the mountain, which had been riddled with mine shafts, began to crumble and collapse into the water. Within a matter of days the town at the foot of the mountain had all but disappeared in the deluge.

When evening came the island, including the palace, had sunk beneath the waves and the people had drowned. Vincent stayed in his boat weeping. He wondered how it was that no one else on the island had known what was going on under their very noses. His heart was heavy as he hoisted sail and set a course for the Mainland.

SOUL CROWS – A MEMORY

WE DIDN'T MIND BROTHER WRAFTER; he didn't bother us much except for the odd ass's bite, but his hand didn't stray much above the thigh. A small man with long greying hair and uncut fingernails, he taught art and music, was a bit operatic for the times, and was inclined to look down on those whose sensibilities were less refined than his own – which really meant everyone in the town.

He swept into the classroom one afternoon in September, grabbed a stick of chalk and drew a staircase on the blackboard – eight treads and eight risers. We thought it was going to be a drawing class but became less sure when he put the letter 'd' on the first tread, 'r' on the second, 'm' on the third and so on up to the top landing where he put another 'd'. We were thoroughly confused by the final product which looked as follows:

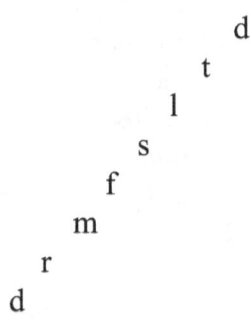

He savoured our bafflement for a while and then said, "This, boys, is the tonic solfa, the foundation of all music and harmony. This is a language. You hear it every day but you don't understand the grammar."

We weren't all that much wiser, and the tough nuts at the back of the class began to groan and punch each other, twisting and turning in their creaking desks.

"Quiet! You bogmen at the back." Then, from beneath the heavy drapery of his habit Wrafter produced a strange looking instrument he called a tuning fork. He knocked it sharply against the edge of the nearest desk and listened intently to the vibrations, his eyes fixed on a definite part of the ceiling.

" M m m m m m m n n n n n d o o o o o o h … Mmmmnnnndooooh … Dooooooooh…" His face was screwed up in concentration and near ecstasy while his needlelike nostrils dilated slightly. Several whispered taunts drifted forward on chalk dust from the back of the room but Wrafter was dead to them. Having fixed the low DO in his musical memory, he went up and down the scales in a quavering contralto. It was our turn next and he willed us up and down that stairway, using the tuning fork as a baton. We, mainly townies, in the front rows tried our best, but the country lads at the back were grimly silent apart from the occasional snigger or mispronunciation of the Holy Name. They would have to put up with another forty minutes of this before escaping to the green swards for hurling practice. A big farm lad called Reville rested his head on his arms, sighed, and wished his life away.

"Give every note its full value," Brother Wrafter instructed. "And I don't want to hear any half notes. Neeeeeeeyyyyyyyy…" He gave an example of an interdicted half-note. "Remember, each proper note is a *full* step up or down from its nearest neighbour."

He had put the tuning fork away for the moment and was using a large wooden compass for conducting.

A little while later he divided us up into four separate groups. One group sang low DO, another, MI, the next, SO, and the final, high DO. Then he rearranged the groupings. I ended up in low DO and my pal, James Masterson, was put in the high DO group. Then all four groups were enjoined to sing their respective notes *together*.

And harmony was born – or at least it was our first encounter with it.

It may not have been such a revelation for James Masterson, who played the accordion and who, we would discover later, had a perfect ear. But he had never until that moment heard of the tonic solfa or the steps that lay behind harmony. Brother Wrafter looked at us as if he had seen some new awareness in our faces. No one could deny it: we had learnt something. And we had learnt it by doing. Whether it was important or not, or whether it would equip us for a job, was another matter.

"Well? Well, boys? You know what that was, don't you? That good sweet sound? That was harmony. What was it?"

"Harmony, Sir."

"The harmony of the spheres. I'll tell you about that some time. Even in this grubby little town you can reach for the stars, for something of the Divine, if you've got harmony." His scrawny arms, bared as the sleeves of the habit fell back, reached out towards the window that gave on to the town dump.

"What a load of shite…" It had to have come from Reville at the back of the class, but the Maestro was too wound up and enmeshed in cosmological proportions to hear.

Wrafter told us of his intention to form a choir which would be called, 'The Hosannas'.

"Over the next few weeks I'll be auditioning for the choir."

After the class Reville started to push James Masterson around. "I suppose you're going to be one of Wrafter's choirboys. The Hosannas…"

"I hope so. I like music. Maybe you'll get in as well." James could fight his corner when the need arose. "I'll give you grinds if you like."

Reville swung at him. "Shag off, Masterson, you little Nancy boy." The tough nuts followed him out laughing. One of them expressed the view that all townies were Nancy boys whether they were Hosannas or not. They all laughed again. Humour didn't have to be very subtle to amuse them.

The auditions went on for two weeks. Each one of us in turn had to go to the top of the class and sing a piece of music Wrafter taught us. It was called 'Bella Signora' and it spanned two octaves or more. None of us had ever heard of it before or since. The first line went something like: "Bel...la...Sig...no...o...o...o...o...o... o...o...o...o...ra." It started high, a lot higher than the tuning fork, and went higher still, reaching a peak at the third 'o'. Then it all went down the stairs to a very low DO indeed. Perhaps there were even three flights of stairs in it. Not surprisingly James Masterson was the best and he was chosen immediately for the choir. Most of the front rows did all right and I just about scraped in.

The interesting thing was that the back rows all failed the audition to a man. Reville's rendition of 'Bella Signora' was like a series of drunken roars you might hear in the Irishtown on a Friday night. Most of the atrocious performances were deliberate; it was clear that none of the tough nuts wanted to be one of Wrafter's Hosannas. In fact they were terrified of such an outcome. As soon as each one of them finished his audition Brother Wrafter would remove his hands from his ears and shout, "Crow!" He would point to the benches that were placed on the periphery of the class and each crow would go, often grinning, to take his place on one of the safe benches where they were supposed to do some homework but never did.

Those of us who earned a place in the choir were divided into 'Firsts' and 'Seconds' depending on how we coped with the high and low notes. I was glad to be in the 'Seconds' because having a lowish voice removed some of the cissy stigma, though not all. James didn't mind being a 'First' and in retrospect I realise that he was probably the bravest of us all.

The first song we learnt was 'The Barcarole'. Wrafter had the words all written out on a roll of wallpaper which he draped over the blackboard. Words for the 'Firsts' were in blue, the 'Seconds' red. Over each line were the notes, DO, RE, MI, etc.

The Maestro would start by giving the tuning fork a good whack; then he would sing the first note to cue in the 'Firsts'. He would raise the wooden compass aloft and hold it there until he was satisfied that he had the attention of every member of the choir. Then he would bring his baton down sharply and the 'Firsts' were off and running, like greyhounds out of the traps:

"Night of stars and ni … ght of love … flow ge … en … tly o'er the wa … ter…"

Just after 'water' we, the 'Seconds', would come in, repeating the line in a lower register, while the 'Firsts' went off and up on a solo run. They led and we followed but we were important too because we anchored them and without us there would have been no harmony, only melody. To this day, I don't know the melody of 'The Barcarole', only the 'Seconds' part. We had to shut our ears to the 'Firsts' or we would be distracted and go astray, maybe even follow *their* part.

James was the exception. He could change from one part to the other and back again without turning a hair and he often did just that in the same rendition. Whether Wrafter knew what he was doing was unclear. But since James would only change to the other part if he felt it needed strengthening, he probably added to the unity of the whole piece. But what was even more remarkable was that James sometimes invented completely new and more elaborate harmonies, none of which was written on the wallpaper. And they all worked perfectly. He was a natural.

But he often put me astray with his extemporising. I would be listening to what he was doing and lose my own part. Whenever that happened I could never get back on track and would have to stop, though keeping my mouth open as if I were singing.

Sometimes the crows, seated along the perimeter line would try to distract us by throwing paper pellets or ball bearings at us when we were in full cry. Once, when a missile hit James on the back of the head, the Maestro brought us to a sudden halt, marched straight to Reville, lifted him up by the ear and threw him out of the classroom, muttering, "Ignoramus …

Philistine ... Bogman..." He seemed to be searching for the right word. Then he remembered it. "You crow. Out, out damned CROW!" The Hosannas began to feel just a little bit special.

Wrafter explained to us how the Spartans, the hardest men in history, used to remove strings from their lyres because they thought music, especially sweet music, softened men up. Eventually of course they were beaten by the Athenians, who loved music. The moral of the story was obvious.

Even today, he went on, hard men followed the image of the strong silent type, epitomised on the cinema screen by Gary Cooper. But, he quickly pointed out, that economy with words was also a false economy and could lead to problems of misunderstanding. His lower lip trembled when he said that. We had no idea why.

The choir grew in confidence and we got to know the signs and signals of the Maestro, and could even read the expressions in his pink face as he waved the compass about. It wasn't exactly like playing a match but it was a sort of team nevertheless. Two-part harmony was ambitious enough for us in those days before the country discovered and started to explore its amazingly rich musical heritage.

On one fine afternoon with sun warming the windowpanes, something happened. It all fell into place, the notes, melody, parts, rhythm. And James was doing something completely new which worked like a charm. He would go off on a solo run of grace notes and then at the right moment would come looping back to the melody. It all flowed. Wrafter's face grew pinker with excitement as he conducted with the wooden compass. He was tense as well, as if afraid something might happen to spoil the moment. He glanced occasionally at the crows on the sidelines to make sure they were behaving themselves. We were half way through 'The Barcarole' when he said in a loud whisper in time with the rhythm, "I'll ... tell ... you ... some ... thing ... lat ... er."

His arm movements became more subtle. He tamped down the 'Firsts', who were becoming a little too enthusiastic, and brought us up. Strands of grey hair fell over his damp forehead. We were surrounded by a good sound. Nothing could go wrong. We had it nailed. It was better than beating Enniscorthy by three goals. We could hardly believe that we were making this sound. It was like something you might hear on the radio. And it all started with the tonic solfa.

When, at last, the Maestro brought the compass down there was a short silence. He produced a handkerchief from the pocket where he kept the leather, and wiped his gleaming face.

"That was good, boys, very good. What I wanted to tell you is this." He waited for a while and looked at the lines of crows, then he shouted excitedly, "EVEN THE CROWS WERE SINGING!" He threw his fist into the air.

It was true. Some of them had at least been humming along and most had been swaying to the tempo. The crows looked up in shock as if they'd been insulted. Wrafter smiled at them – probably for the first time ever – and said, "Yes, Reville, even you."

Brother Wrafter died in his sleep almost three years after our class finished the Leaving Certificate. Reville, who had inherited his father's farm, went into the cattle business and lived well – mainly on agricultural grants and subsidies coming from Brussels. On the rare occasions I ran into him he would try to embarrass me about having been a "DO-RE-MI cissy." All that came to an end when I moved to Dublin to work in the civil service and, implicitly, put security ahead of excitement.

James Masterson tried to get on in the world of music but no band or group wanted to hire an accordion-player, however gifted, after the electric guitar had come into fashion. He emigrated to the United States where he enlisted in the army and fought in Vietnam. He died during the Tet Offensive. An unconfirmed report said the cause was friendly fire, but there were rumours that he had deliberately walked on a mine. He was only twenty-two. I missed him then and I miss him now.

I suppose Brother Wrafter didn't really equip us very well for the practicalities of life. But we learned something from him; even the crows absorbed the rudiments of harmony while perched along the wall of the classroom in the fading yellow of that autumn's sun.

THE LANGUAGE OF TREES

WHERE DOES IT EVER BEGIN, what is the true origin of the process that leads inexorably to the point of separation? Presumably there had been signs, there must have been signs, straws in the wind, though scarcely discernible in the swirling chaff. One argument came to John's mind as a candidate for 'the last straw', though it could have been one of a thousand. He couldn't even remember the cause of the argument, the issue. Had it been something stupid to do with politics or religion or maybe it had been about the children? In any case he couldn't recall the subject, only the shape of the exchange, the way they circled around the vortex, being drawn deeper and deeper in. They must have collided in the process, because there were scars to show for it, scars that this time didn't heal.

The structure would have been something like the following:

"So, you agree with me then," Ruth probably challenged.

"No, but I sympathise with your point of view." John holding whatever ground he'd won but trying to be conciliatory.

"Don't patronise me."

"I'm not. I respect what you're saying. I just don't agree with it."

"That doesn't make sense."

"Yes, it does."

"How can it possibly make sense? It's either right or wrong."

"Not wrong exactly – partial, incomplete. Other things have to be taken into account. It's just not that simple."

"So, it's too complicated for me. That's what you're saying, you bastard."

Maybe that was the shape of the final wrench. But surely it wasn't enough to lead to the enormity of losing his marriage and his children. A contributory factor maybe, well undoubtedly. One of many bouts that left them reeling, seeking neutral corners. The trouble about misunderstandings is that sometimes there's no way back; words don't exist independently anymore, only the speakers who impart those meanings that have come to be expected. The origin is lost, the words are ice floes sliding by, melting into warmer tides.

Now in his mid-fifties, John walked on his own through the wood where he used to bring the children. It was a real wood, not a Scandinavian forest of isosceles pines, but full of old bent oaks, beech and ash, all bursting at the seams, criss-crossing each other, trunks strangled with ivy. Rotting lichen-covered branches lay half-hidden in the mulchy fern-filled soil, and many an uprooted tree lay at an angle, dying against its neighbours, but prevented from falling completely by the crush of new growth springing up from the ageless carpet of pine needles and the debris of innumerable autumns. Death and rebirth were everywhere in evidence in a chaotic jumble, and yet there was an order somewhere behind it all. In summer, astounding shafts of sunlight penetrated in inexplicable ways.

Once, he and the kids noticed a small sycamore sapling trying to put down roots in a rocky area. Using his pocket-knife, John, watched intently by the kids, replanted it in better soil. Before leaving it, he saw that the fresh earth was covering a tiny little shoot on the main stem. He freed and cleaned it, observing that when the tree was fully grown that little shoot would be a branch close enough to the ground for children to play on. The three faces of his children studied the toothpick-sized shoot, marvelling at the potential it contained. He would never forget those expressions of deep wonder. He mused aloud whether he would still be around when the tree matured. The kids looked silently at him, then back at the sapling.

———————

Memories like these crowded into his head as he sat on a rock to eat his sandwich. Opposite him was the sycamore tree, now about ten feet tall and thriving. The tiny shoot had grown into a branch the size of a human arm.

He reckoned he was becoming eccentric, sometimes rehearsing conversations in his mind, hoping that part of them didn't slip out aloud. He spoke to his children under his breath, remembering the small hands in his, the dented little ski-caps they wore. Where were they now, at this moment? He had no idea. He ached for those years back again. The wood enfolded him. He thought the world would end when all the woods on the planet looked exactly like this one. There was no one to contradict him.

THE SLEEP OF THE JUST

WE HAD GEM FOR MATHS and Irish. He was not so much old as ancient, having reached the stage where time encrusts, much as it does coral. He had gone beyond the age of feebleness, and had grown scaly and impregnable, like a prehistoric alligator. His ideas about teaching had probably not changed for fifty years; but then they were good, common-sense ideas to start with. He commanded respect and attention; no pupil could have dealt lightly with that igneous face which sometimes softened into a red indignant craw, over which his collar stud rode roughshod. His eyes, peering over half-glasses, glinted like mica, and missed absolutely nothing.

The top of his head was completely flat, as if some ceiling had curtailed his growth, giving him also a slight stoop, and his white bristly hair had no option but to jut forward over his forehead. When he thought, or rather cogitated, over some problem he screwed his face into a sort of carved African mask while he scratched his head, sending puffs of dandruff flying into sunlight. Long gone were worries about self-image or what people thought. These overlays had long since been weathered away.

In the afternoons he would sit in the sun and teach while the chalk dust floated in the sunbeam coming from the window behind the blackboard. His teaching of Irish had a healthy disrespect for grammar or curriculum. He told stories in such a way that the language came alive. They were not merely translations of English stories; the meaning was as distinctly Irish as the words and idioms themselves.

The matter and form blended in a natural way. Gem used to argue that it was just as well the Renaissance had passed Ireland by because it would have altered the spirit of the language and of the life-affirming Brehon culture. Being an island race, it was our nature to exaggerate, to make things larger than life. Nothing should be accepted or seen at face value, that way lay poverty of spirit, a very English trait. What was required was the soaring imagination of blind poets and bards who made ingenious literary artefacts of praise, satire and lament.

"There are still people in the West," Gem mused in flowing Irish, "who cannot tell one word of the truth, God bless them. One of them, a small farmer, told me a story of a chicken he had for his dinner. It was no ordinary chicken. Oh no, it certainly was not. He and his wife and their five children had it for their dinner one Sunday. It sat in the middle of the table and he could not see the rest of the family over the top of it. He himself had to stand on the flour box to carve it. On the Monday the harvest started and his wife fed the whole *meitheal* of men on the bird until all four fields were cut and threshed. When eventually the bones and ribcage of this magnificent bird began to show through, he thought for one moment that he was looking at a cathedral. What would you think of a bird like that, Daly?"

"A great bird, Sir."

"And a great man," said Gem, "who could carve it as well as concoct it."

And so it went on, sessions of pointed anecdotes and colour, inducing a state of utter concentration. I remember how the whole class used to settle itself before he commenced. Then there was the hypnotic effect of regular breathing, combined with the after-dinner feeling of satisfaction. The outside world faded away; the only extraneous activity consisted of probing a bit of grist caught between teeth or shooing a wasp, but even these were almost unconscious actions. In one way we seemed to be on the borders of sleep but our minds were doubly alert. The particles in the sunbeam seemed to trigger the imagination. There was a good feeling of being able to think through any problem from first principles without having to resort to rules and conventions. There was also a sort of fulfilment in pushing thought back as far as it would go, right to the font. The process of thought became an end in itself.

Being a maths teacher too, he clearly had a feeling for the exactitude of symbols but he really seemed to get more mileage out of the slipperiness of words – which, in his view, illustrated rather than defined. He believed that the process of real understanding was not always a logical one.

"You don't know what the word 'leamh' means, Sinnot. Suppose you had a blue duck egg and a pig's foot and the juice was running down your chin, but you did not have any salt or a dash of raspberry what would it be?"

"What would what be, Sir?"

"The general effect, Sinnot. Deduce the general effect of this dainty collation... All right, I'll tell you. It would be insipid. 'Leamh' means insipid. What does it mean?"

"In ... sipp ... it, Sir."

"And what does that mean?"

"It means... It's like when you have no salt in an egg, Sir."

"Stand out in the line." Gem then proceeded to ask the others who also failed and who found themselves in the line behind Sinnot.

One by one, Gem cradled the contrite cheeks in his left hand and slowly drew back his left hand, intoning, "Shall I this priceless gem destroy?" (It was from this phrase that he got his nickname). The right hand began its descent very quickly as the waiting face cringed in anticipation and Gem bared his gapped teeth in a devilish grin. Just before the blow fell there was a sudden deceleration so that what was to be a ferocious clout ended up as not much more than a pat on the cheek.

The lack of pain never ceased to surprise, even though the rite was repeated three times for everybody. Looking back, the 'three wops', as it was called, really didn't have a punitive element at all and seemed to have had an almost spiritual significance like the laying on of hands; or of an old teacher transmitting his blessing to the young. Whatever it was, it conferred the gift of total recall. Words such as 'leamh' were never forgotten.

At some point we heard that Gem's only daughter had died young from cancer and we noticed that he began to drink heavily. On one occasion those of us who were taking higher maths were gathered in a semicircle behind the blackboard for a private session with Gem. His figures wandered on the board and he seemed to be supporting himself on the easel. Sinnot caught my eye, feigned a hiccup and sniggered. Gem whirled round, lost his balance and the blackboard came crashing down. There was a deadly silence as Gem composed himself. We looked down at the fallen blackboard as if an altar had just been ransacked.

"Pick it up and rub it out," Gem said to me. I reassembled the blackboard and rubbed until it shone like ebony.

"Sinnot, please tell the class what nought diyided by nought is," Gem said.

" Em ... nought I suppose, Sir," Sinnot stammered.

"Mr. Sinnot tells us the answer is nought; the symbol of eternal recurrence... Not a bad guess where rules conflict and there are no signposts. But the confidence of youth must be tested...

Draw for us without aid of compass the perfect nought. Give him the chalk."

Sinnot checked to see if Gem was serious and then began to draw a large circle. His first attempt was way off but Gem painstakingly checked it with the blackboard compass.

"I said a circle, not your Granny's cat. If Giotto could draw a perfect circle freehand, surely Sinnot of Brogue Street can do likewise?"

"It's hard Sir."

"It is hard. So what does failure really mean? Is it the inability to draw a circle or the inability to … carry a cross?"

The air seemed wounded. Sinnot could make no reply, but stood looking down at his feet, chalk in hand. Gem looked at the latest attempt on the board out of his bloodshot eyes and said wearily, "Sit down, boy."

Shortly afterwards Gem went on sick leave. Some said it was to take the cure. The exams drew near and we began to worry about the part of the maths course that we had not covered. One evening a few of us worked on a likely problem in calculus, but without success. Daly's hair stood on end from repeated tearing and Sinnot's acne was bleeding in spots from similar gestures of frustration.

"It just won't come out this way," Daly shouted.

"God Almighty, we tried it every other way," Sinnot put in. "There's only one thing for it. We'll have to bring it down to Gem in his house."

"Not me," I said, but after tossing a coin, it was.

His house was a converted butcher's shop with the large window and fascia board intact. Under the paint of the fascia board you could just make out the word *Flesher*. Inside the big window were pots of aspidistra and rubber plants around which a few cats curled in sleep in the surrounding gloom. This was the house Gem had left every morning for fifty years before climbing the steep hill to the school. He would take the steps one at a time, putting both feet on each step and reassuring himself of his balance before taking the next step. One hand held the railing, the other the inevitable Woodbine. The steps of the hill were always chalked on by the local children, and Gem studied the various drawings and scribbles with consummate interest. Most of the 'artists' would probably have been through his hands at one time or another and he could probably identify them from their style. Was there something of himself in those markings, those innocent scribbles before the era of graffiti?

It was hard to comprehend his daily pilgrimage which lasted for half a century or more. Could some of the hollowness of the steps be attributed to his feet alone? Was he ever young enough to eschew the steps and canter up the gradient as the children did?

I confronted the door-knocker for a long

time, feeling intimidated about bearding this lion in his den. The house itself seemed to cast a shadow on the animation of the street, where women wheeled laden prams, loafers emerged noisily from pubs, and the fish women shooed gulls away from their stalls of herring and mackerel.

A tentative knock brought Gem to the door. But he was no lion disturbed from sleep. He seemed small and frail inside a crumpled dressing gown, and the gloom lodged in the lines and hollows of his face. There seemed to be a spirit in that house that diminished people.

"Oh, it's you," he muttered.

I put my case, adding in justification, "The exams are only two weeks off."

"Exams?" he queried, as if they had not been part of his stock in trade for half a century. "What's the point?" he added to himself.

"I'm sorry Sir. I shouldn't have bothered you at home," I said, unable to keep a note of surprise out of my voice.

He looked at me for a long time.

"You're going in for the County Scholarship?" he inquired.

"Yes, Sir."

Gem reminisced briefly about his own University days, about rag week and faculty dances and conferring ceremonies. There was a moment when we spoke as friends, almost as contemporaries with the same aspirations. The moment didn't last; maybe his dreams were spent.

He didn't solve the maths problem then, but he returned to school the following week and helped us with the rest of the syllabus. He was still drinking and it was obvious to all that the required effort of concentration was taking it out of him.

The exams went on for a fortnight that Summer and the only sunlight we saw was criss-crossed by window panes as if it was being parcelled out. We suffered all the excruciating effects of utter concentration. Once a sparrow flew in the window and around the classroom; its ejection by the very formal Superintendent drew hardly a smile. The last paper was easily the most difficult. It was the door to freedom but it still took three hours to push it open, answer by answer, and line by line. And then, unbelievably, it was open and the holidays – and the future – flooded in.

During the exams, Gem was to be seen wandering around the quays most evenings until sunset, watching the occasional ship come in, or the eel fishermen casting their lines, or the old men sitting on benches cutting plug tobacco. He didn't talk much, or try to interpret chalk scribbles, or make a bridge hand out of car registration numbers. When it was time, he retired into the dark cavern of his home.

But he did convene us afterwards for a post mortem on the exam. This was no ordeal. We were the successful gladiators returning to the

Colosseum of our own free will. We met in a corner of the old classroom. Having gone through the maths papers and satisfied himself that we had done all right, he turned to the Irish papers, mocking the unoriginality of some of the questions. One of the essays was 'Why I like autumn'. Sinnot said he had chosen to do that one and, in response to a question from Gem, said that he had focused on the idea of acceptance.

Gem began to reflect aloud. Somehow he was sitting in the sunbeam again, and ideas floated as prolifically as chalk dust. He refused to accept autumn as the season of acceptance.

His breathing became shallow. He slept for a while and his head dropped to his chest and he sat there in the last rays of the sun.

THE TOWER

AT FIRST THE WIND was a comforting sound and Brendan didn't mind lying awake listening to it, even when it made the ivy on the outside of the house scratch against the bedroom windows. His partner, Martina, was asleep beside him; her breathing was much softer than the wind and much more regular. She was a terrific sleeper; he doubted if a hurricane could wake her.

The wind came in unpredictable waves that reached a crescendo, then died away for a while. During the lulls he was conscious of waiting for the next wave and then the one after that. He had the impression that they were growing in volume and frequency; there was less shape to them. They had become wilder, more like squalls. Somehow, there was a loss of control and he no longer felt comforted by the sounds as they whipped around the gable, sometimes with the whine of a cable snapping. There was some extraordinary force behind the leading edge that whistled through the night. It was as if nature was in pain. Was it his mother who used to say a storm was the sound of souls in hell?

Although fast asleep, Martina stirred a few times, once inquiring incoherently why he was still awake.

"It's all right," he said.

But when he heard a roof tile hitting the ground he knew it wasn't all right. It was *his* roof and he had supervised its construction himself only two years ago. Suddenly, he realised there was far more at stake. The tower! He sat bolt upright. He recalled it quite clearly on his drawing table. What safety margin had he allowed for in the design? Pressure from clients and architects had forced engineers like himself to pare these margins to the bone.

As he got out of bed Martina turned petulantly away, bringing his share of the duvet with her. He went to his study and rummaged through filing cabinets until he found the drawing of 'the tower', so-called by the architect in an attempt to gentrify a chimney stack. He went over the calculations again and confirmed his recollection: maximum wind speed tolerance 130 miles per hour and that of course was based on the assumption that the clerk of works had properly supervised the quality of the cement and the bricklaying. He rang the Met Service to learn that the freak gales were already gusting in the region of 110 miles per hour and were likely to increase over the coming hours.

He froze with fear. Even though he'd built within the prescribed safety margins, he would be blamed if the tower collapsed. He had professional insurance and he felt sure it covered acts of God, but that wasn't the point. A structural failure so early in his career would ruin his reputation. He had a vision of the tower being blown over and falling in slow motion, sending up clouds of dust and debris. This was followed by a much worse scenario: the tower falling on some of the nearby houses. How close were the houses? He had never fully understood how the Trade Centre towers had fallen so neatly into their footprints, doing little collateral damage. His tower would fall sideways even though there were structural steel columns.

He went to the same filing cabinet and found an aerial photograph of the site. He scaled and measured it. The results were grim: if the tower fell to the north or west several artisans' dwellings would be crushed; many of them housed large families.

He crept unsteadily upstairs and brought his clothes out to the landing, where he dressed as quickly as he could. In the short distance to the car in the driveway the wind nearly took his feet from under him. It was worse than he thought. The same feeling of powerlessness overcame him as he felt the car being buffeted by the wind as he drove towards the site. Tree branches and electric wires were down, a rubble wall had collapsed and some metal traffic signs were bent double. As he got closer to the site he was conscious of an acute pain in his shoulder blades; he had been craning his neck in hopes of seeing the top of the tower over the surrounding roofs.

Finally, and to his great relief, it came into view. He parked about 200 metres away. Even from there he could see that there was a degree of sway at the top of the tower. From the back of the car he got a theodolite and some other instruments which he fixed to a tripod. When he'd finished his measurements he was seized again by panic. It was balanced on a knife edge. Cracks could appear at any moment.

Panic drove him to action. He called the police on his mobile and explained the situation as best he could, identifying two areas of housing where he thought evacuation would be necessary.

"I see… And could I have your name, Sir?" the desk sergeant asked.

"There's no time for all that," Brendan said breathlessly. "I'm not a crank. This is serious." He rang off.

As he drove home be tried to reassure himself that the ball was in their court now. He had reported it to the authorities; what more could he do? The monkey was off his back, or was it? He gagged a couple of times and eventually had to stop on the hard shoulder to throw up; the wind, which was even stronger now, blew most of his stomach contents all over him.

When he got home he showered and slipped into bed. It was 4.30 a.m. Martina muttered something in her sleep which he couldn't understand. He stared at the ceiling until the first light began to filter through the curtains. He had done all that he could do. The tower would stand or it would fall. If it fell it would be an act of God. He could hardly be blamed for that.

He switched on the radio to get the first news

bulletin of the day. *The freak storm that raged all night caused serious damage in many parts of the country. There was considerable loss of life in the following areas...*

He switched it off, turned sideways and drew his knees up under his chin. He rocked gently.

ZEUS

"ARE YOU SURE you don't want to keep him yourself?" Nelly asked Sophie as the new dog – a Springer Spaniel – looked around the unfamiliar kitchen.

"No," Sophie said, "we got a new pup and we'd like you to have this fella. He'll be great with the kids."

The two women had a cup of tea in the kitchen, their chat interrupted every now and again by some interesting item on the radio.

That evening there was great excitement in the kitchen as the family gathered around the dog. The kids christened him 'Zeus' after a dog on a TV show. Their father, Thomas, explained that it was a pure-bred all-purpose hunting dog which would have to be exercised regularly.

Cross-examined by the kids, he went on to explain that pointers point and retrievers retrieve but the Springer Spaniel does both. "Of course," he concluded "we don't shoot birds and that's why we'll have to exercise him in different ways, throwing sticks and so on."

In the following few days they acquired all the appropriate accoutrements, a leash with choke chain, a collar with name tag and phone number, a dish with inward sloping sides to prevent the floppy ears from falling into the food, a wire-bristled grooming comb and various toys and rubber bones. Zeus would be one well cared for family pet.

They brought him out for the traditional Sunday drive and as they scampered down the sand dunes towards the sea, Thomas said, "Now kids, you'll see how Zeus takes to the water. He's a hunting dog so it's his nature. It's been bred into him over hundreds of years. This should be interesting to watch."

They tried everything but it soon became clear there was no way the dog was going next or near the water. He didn't even like the sand, and started to retch after sniffing a pile of seaweed. They threw sticks for a while but Zeus paid no attention and moped around, snuffling in the sand.

"Hmmm, this bears thinking about," Thomas said, his theories in disarray.

Over the following weeks it turned out that Zeus was not a happy animal. He hated being groomed and on several occasions when Thomas tried to get the tangles out of his ears, the dog turned sharply and snapped at him. Worse was to follow.

Nelly brought him to the shops on Saturday and left him tied up outside the supermarket. When she came out of the store she discovered to her horror that Zeus had attacked a smaller dog – a wiry little mongrel – whose owner was distraught. Nelly apologised and told the other person to send her the vet's bill.

"I don't think we can trust him around the children," Nelly said when she got him home.

"Maybe he needs a little more training." Thomas folded up a newspaper and diffidently swiped it across Zeus's snout. After a few modest passes, Zeus grabbed the newspaper in his jaws and shredded it.

Other eccentricities emerged. Zeus ate tissues and swallowed socks, later puking them up. He continued to attack smaller dogs whenever he got the chance. "He's a bully," Thomas thought, but then realised it was wrong to attribute human motivation to animals. Still, it struck him as odd that Zeus never went for big dogs but was in fact inclined to slink away from them.

The vet didn't hold out much hope of rehabilitation. "Castration probably wouldn't help," he said. "He may have been attacked by another dog when he was a pup. Or else he's overbred. Springer Spaniels can be unpredictable at the best of times."

"Oh?" Thomas wasn't thrilled by this news.

"In thirty years' practice," the vet continued, "I was bitten once and that was by a Springer Spaniel." He looked at Thomas. "Did you get him as a pup?"

"No. A friend of the wife's gave him to us a couple of months ago."

"I see," the vet said.

Thomas began to see too. "You don't think … he was … dumped on us?"

"It's happened before. You might've been sold a pup, as they say."

They agreed to give Zeus one last chance.

During that reprieve Thomas walked him one Saturday morning, keeping him on the leash. They went to the park where there was a soccer game in progress. Standing on the sidelines they watched the match for a while, listening to the barracking and urgent shouts of encouragement coming from the supporters. The dog behaved quite well and didn't strain against the leash.

The park was virtually deserted when Thomas turned for home. He decided to let Zeus off the leash and have a run around. Zeus took off at speed, chasing autumn leaves, sniffing shrubbery, raising his leg against trees – all normal doggy things. Maybe he would turn out all right, Thomas thought. Vets had to look at the downside to protect their reputations.

Suddenly, Zeus darted to his right and disappeared around the corner of a pathway. Thomas wasn't unduly concerned until he heard the screams, human screams. His heart lurched. He started to run.

As he turned the corner he saw Zeus with a small dog in his jaws. There was blood everywhere. The dog's owner, an elderly woman, was leaning back against a wall, screaming.

"It's all right," Thomas shouted, trying to reassure himself as much as her.

"Do something…!" she begged.

He grabbed Zeus viciously by the neck and squeezed hard. He had some notion that if he choked him he would have to open his jaws and release the poodle. It didn't work. The poodle had stopped yapping now and was on the point of passing out … or dying. The woman continued to scream. Thomas was afraid she would have a heart attack. He was also afraid he would have a heart attack.

In desperation he plunged his fingers into Zeus's bloody jaws. But try as he might, he could not prize them apart. He punched the animal about the head but this had the effect of making the poodle bleed even more.

Then he had an inspiration. He moved to a position a few yards behind Zeus. From a running start he swung his right foot upwards, between the dog's hind legs, and kicked him hard in the testicles. The two dogs rose about two feet in the air. Zeus let out a howl of pain and as he did so the poodle dropped from his jaws and scampered towards its mistress. Thomas gave Zeus another kick for good measure and sent him on his way. He apologised profusely to the woman and told her to send him the vet's bill. He used his handkerchief to clean the wounds. Now that the incident was over and her beloved pooch was still alive, the woman recovered reasonably quickly, to the point where she managed to give Thomas a piece of her mind.

"I told you there was something wrong with that dog," Nelly said.

"He's mad." Thomas said, looking out the kitchen window at Zeus, who stood trembling, his eyes completely bloodshot. "My God, look at his eyes. It's not natural."

"I'll never forgive Sophie for foisting him on us," Nelly said. "I can't believe she did that, knowing the ages of our kids and everything. The bitch."

"Well, she's not going to take him back. We're going to have to bring him to the Dogs and Cats Home."

They told the kids that Zeus was going to a better home. They all helped gather up his belongings; dish, leash, grooming comb, etc. They all piled into the car.

"I think he knows we're dumping him," one of the kids said.

"We're not dumping him" Thomas replied. "They'll find him a more suitable home." He gave a sidelong glance at Nelly, who kept her eyes firmly on the road ahead. Zeus was unusually quiet and docile, almost as if he sensed he had run out of chances. But then he had never been exactly frisky. In fact he always seemed put upon in some strange way.

"I still can't believe Sophie deliberately ... you know..." Nelly didn't finish it because of the kids.

"Oh maybe it wasn't deliberate as such..." Thomas began.

"In a pig's eye."

"What's a pig's eye, Mam?" a voice from the back of the car inquired.

"It's just an expression..."

As they were leading Zeus out of the car at

the Dogs and Cats Home, an elderly woman approached them. She carried a placard which read "Animals Have Rights".

"Oh God," Thomas groaned.

The woman wasn't a fanatic however, indeed she seemed quite reasonable. She told them that if they put their pet in the home he would be sent to Trinity College lab to be experimented on.

"Oh, now..." Nelly demurred.

"It's true," the woman insisted. "My daughter is married to a lab technician."

Thomas briefly explained the problems they had with the dog and how they had no option.

"There's a vet in Ballsbridge who specialises in problem cases," the woman said. "Even if there's no cure he might be able to place him down the country where he couldn't do any harm." She gave them the vet's address.

Thomas looked at Nelly who looked at the kids. They all looked at Zeus, who didn't look at anyone.

"I suppose we could try that," Nelly said.

They drove back to Ballsbridge and located the vet, who saw them after a slight delay. He listened to their story and shook his head.

"That woman has me pestered," he said. "I can't work miracles. That dog would cause mayhem down the country, worrying cattle and sheep. He'd be shot or drowned in a bog hole within a week."

"Maybe he needs to hunt," Thomas put in. "He is a gun dog after all."

"From what you told me," the vet said, "I can't really see him retrieving any birds. He'd shred them to pieces. No. I'm afraid he's just faulty. A bad gene maybe. Or a bad experience when he was a pup. I'll put him down humanely if you like."

Nelly looked at Zeus, who was chewing on a seat belt. She declined the offer. They got in the car and drove back to the Dogs and Cats Home. Mercifully, the animal rights woman was missing, perhaps gone for her lunch.

Fighting back tears, the children said good bye to Zeus and said they'd come to visit him often.

Inside the home, which smelled like the monkey house in the zoo and was rent by animal sounds of different pitch and stridency, Thomas explained the situation to a middle-aged official who sat at a sort of reception desk.

"Here's his dish and grooming comb," Nelly placed the articles on the desk.

"That's grand," the man said, barely noticing them. He called a helper who took the leash from Thomas's hand and began to lead Zeus away.

"Good bye, old fella," Nelly said, patting the dog on the head. She watched as he was led down a straw-littered corridor and put in a wire-mesh cage. It was like committing a relative to an insane asylum.

"You ... em ... don't send them to the lab in Trinity...?" Thomas inquired.

"No," the man replied. "I see Bridie has been

bending your ear?"

"And you … keep them…?" Nelly followed up.

"Oh yeah … for as long as we can."

Thomas handed him a fifty-euro note. "That might help."

"Yes indeed. Much appreciated." The man was no stranger to donations of blood money.

There wasn't much more to be said. They were quiet during the drive home. The deed was done. There was a smell in the car; one of the kids located the source – a small blob of vomit like a spoonful of porridge.

Had Zeus somehow known what was in store? Nelly was under no illusion. They'd probably put him down already. The contribution for bed and board was all a charade, designed to make people feel better, to leave at least some doubt in their minds.

Thomas knew it too. He remembered what the vet had said about a bad gene. He found it hard to accept that any animal was so beyond redemption that he had to be destroyed. Why had he been born?

"Will we visit him tomorrow?" one of the kids asked from the back of the car.

"We'll see, Pet," Nelly said, looking straight ahead. She felt miserable about the kids and about the dog, and she couldn't understand how Sophie had done it to them. She was worse than the dog had ever been.

THE PINK MAN

IT WAS JUST BEFORE CHRISTMAS and Nurse O'Donnell had painted Santas, reindeer, holly and bells on the windows of the Casualty ward, sometimes called the Paupers' ward. The atmosphere was good because everyone was resigned to the fact that they would not be getting out for Christmas; they were all in the same boat. The nurses, too, were aware that they had drawn the short straw and were determined to make the best of the situation. Everyone had grown used to the smell of ether, disinfectant, ammonia and bib dribble.

An elderly man, Mr. Carroll, was recovering from a prostate operation. When the nurses plumped up his pillows he would sit bolt upright in bed, reading the newspaper, his thin grey hair combed back neatly from his forehead. His freshly shaved face would shine with cleanliness and, invariably, there were pink spots in his cheeks, like flowers that bloomed late in the season. Nurse O'Donnell seemed to enjoy sprucing him up, after which she would stand back a few feet appraising her handiwork. Maybe he reminded her of her father or grandfather. But everyone in the ward liked Mr. Carroll; he wasn't witty, nor could he be described as a character. People just found him likeable, one of the dwindling band of nature's gentlemen.

He didn't flirt with the nurses like some of

the other men did, but he would often let them know that his youngest lad was still single and would be regarded as a bit of a catch. Mr. Carroll frequently offered to make the necessary introductions. He seemed especially keen to fix up Nurse O'Donnell with the young lad – who was probably forty if he was a day.

"You'd get on like a house on fire," he'd say to Nurse O'Donnell, who would hoot with laughter and reply that she had a fella of her own, which was hardly true unless she meant the chronic student in the corner bed under the statue of St. Philomena. The curtains around that bed were mysteriously drawn every night after lights out and every man in the ward cocked an envious ear for giggles and other related sounds.

"Well, have ye a friend who needs to be fixed up?" Mr. Carroll would persist.

"Come on now, Mr. Carroll, be a good man and take your pill for me."

Jack McDowell had an infected scrotum. That morning he had been shaved by one of the orderlies, given a pre-op and been taken away singing on a gurney to the operating theatre. He returned to the paupers' ward some two hours later and was now starting to wake up from the anaesthetic. Staff and patients gathered around his bed to listen to his hallucinatory ramblings and they weren't disappointed. Jack cursed like a sailor and betrayed several secrets of the marital chamber in graphic detail. His subconscious was a dark, exotic place like a French port town.

"Now, Mr. McDowell, there's no need to bring Our Lord's name into this," the Matron admonished him while craning forward to hear better. Jack's rantings took a different tack, praising the Lord with considerable irony for blessing him and his poor wife with eight children.

Shortly afterwards, another patient, Sam Mannion, began to come out of a different sort of stupor. He had been indulging himself two nights previously at a Christmas party and become involved in a row, during which he had fallen out of a third storey window. He fell like a baby but unfortunately hit his head against the side of the building on the way down and broke his neck. The ambulance men put sandbags on both sides of his neck to immobilise it and that's how he was brought into casualty and put to bed. Because of the alcohol and the sandbags he hadn't stirred for almost two whole days, during which he was given the hushed respect that is often shown to Egyptian mummies in museums. But now he was beginning to come to with awful retching sounds.

The Matron, who recognised the symptoms of delayed shock, quickly ordered her troops over to his bedside. The curtain was drawn while they worked on him. They had to let him throw up but in a way that didn't sever his spinal cord.

No one in the ward knew how they managed it, but after an hour, the curtains were drawn back, a couple of stainless-steel basins covered with towels were taken away and Sam Mannion was sleeping like a baby, the sandbags replaced by a cervical collar.

"Well done, girls." Mr. Carroll was sitting up in bed with his babyish pink sheen. "Did I tell you that my oldest son, Father Carroll, will be giving a sermon on the radio on Christmas Day?"

"You told us yesterday and..." The Matron didn't have the heart to remind him that he'd told them every day for the last week.

"We'll all be listening in," Nurse O'Donnell said.

"It will be most appropriate for Christmas Day," the Matron added. "You must be very proud of him."

Mr. Carroll gave a babyish, gummy grin, and seemed to shine forth even more brightly than usual. He had finished the newspaper but still sat up straight, staring ahead of him. The snores of Sam Mannion became louder just as the wild ramblings of Jack McDowell faded away. A seven-year-old boy in the bed opposite Mr. Carroll was reading a comic, his leg in traction. The victim of a car accident, he had suffered a bad fracture and there was a large pin through his knee. Patients and visitors sometimes queued up to look at the hole which went right through the plaster of Paris and the bone. The boy liked being the centre of attention until someone gave him a mirror and made him look himself. He set up an awful wail when he saw the vicious looking pin that tunnelled right through his leg. It took Nurse O'Donnell a good half hour of soothing bedside manner to settle him down. Mr. Carroll contributed his two-pence worth by describing bullet holes he had seen in the second world war.

All of the patients were out of anaesthesia and shock when Christmas Day dawned. The Chaplain came to bless them all first thing in the morning and had a Dinky toy for the boy with the hole in his leg. He told Mr. Carroll he was looking forward to his son's sermon later in the day.

After an unusually good breakfast – a rasher as well as the porridge – the surgeons arrived with their wives, dressed in fur coats, and swept through the ward, exchanging pleasantries and spreading seasonal cheer among staff and patients who regarded them with awe. These surgeons or consultants were way above ordinary doctors and were called 'Mister' or 'Professor'; they all had cultivated accents. No one ever really got to talk to them or knew exactly what they did, but everyone knew they were the absolute top of the medical profession, God's anointed ones. While everyone appreciated the visit, there was a slight sense of relief when they left for their mansions in Killiney and Foxrock.

"I'm ready for me sponge bath, Nurse," Jack McDowell sang out. He had recovered well from his operation and, despite some pain where he'd been stitched up, was full of beans.

"No sponge baths today," Nurse O' Donnell told him. "We'll all be listening to Father Carroll on the radio after our dinner."

"I can't wait," someone said with obvious sarcasm, but in a quiet voice so that Mr. Carroll wouldn't hear. He told Nurse O'Donnell he had a Christmas present for her under the bedclothes. If she slipped her hand in she would be able to guess what it was. She quelled him with a look, ignored his comment about the student in the corner bed, and walked briskly away to her station where she pulled a cracker with Matron and won a red paper hat held by a rubber band. The chronic student had been keeping his eye on her and her body language seemed to indicate she would be pulling the curtains around his bed later that night.

The dinner wasn't bad, although the turkey was a bit stringy and the sprouts overcooked. Even Sam Mannion was able to have a forkful or two of breast and mash. There was sponge cake and custard for dessert, followed by cups of tea all round.

After the meal the radio was switched on at high volume so that everyone could hear the sermon being given by Mr. Carroll's son. The sermon dealt with the real meaning of Christmas, the slaughter of the holy innocents by Herod, and the innkeeper who never had a day's peace for the rest of his life. There followed a rendition of

'Silent Night' by the Rathmines and Rathgar Choral Society.

"That was a grand sermon," Sam Mannion opined. "Very deep. Great philosophy in it."

"He's a great theologian and no mistake," Jack McDowell passed along the central aisle of the ward on his way to the bathroom which, since his operation, he was now able to use. "We need more men like him to keep us all on the straight and narrow."

Mr. Carroll accepted these and other plaudits, sitting up in bed, positively aglow. With his good teeth in, his smile lit up the ward. He may even have been a little misty-eyed.

Early on St. Stephen's Day there was a little sleet, not quite snow, but enough like snow to keep people in the Christmas spirit. Through the windows of reindeer and holly the sleet could be seen slanting down at a steep angle; it was a reminder that there was a world outside as well as in. Mr. Carroll was sitting on the side of his bed in his worn but cared-for striped brown suit with lapels as big as elephant ears. The gleaming face, obviously shaved by a cut-throat razor, was set off by a collar and tie which made him seem even more ordered and dapper. His personal belongings were wrapped up in a brown paper parcel which rested in his lap as he waited for his son, the priest, to collect him. Nurse O'Donnell had tied string around the parcel, leaving a finger loop to help him carry it.

"He's coming in his motor car," Mr. Carroll

announced to the ward a few times. "And I'm going to live in his house."

"You'll have the best of everything so," Sam Mannion opined from his still prone position. "Priests know how to look after themselves and their own."

"You never said a truer word," Jack McDowell put in. "What with their housekeepers, buckets of tea on demand, balls of malt and a one-way ticket to the garden of Eden. You have it made, old son."

When the Matron came in to start her rounds she stopped by Mr. Carroll's bed and told him about a phone call she'd just received. It seemed that Father Carroll couldn't come to collect him; something had come up in the parish. But there would be no problem arranging an ambulance for him.

"No ambulance!" Mr. Carroll cried out. "I want my son to collect me." The blood left his cheeks. The Matron and Nurse O' Donnell tried to reason with him. He shook his head, eyes firmly closed. He tried to stand up but tottered back on to the edge of the bed, still clutching the brown parcel. His face sagged; whatever blessing had protected him from his true age was suddenly removed.

"An ambulance will be fine, Mr. Carroll..."

"No ambulance! I want ... my son ... his motor car..." His face coloured but there was no sign of the healthy pink. He began to weep. The ward fell silent as the Matron looked around for help.

Jack McDowell made a diffident attempt. "You'll be grand in an ambulance. Door-to-door service ... couldn't beat it... I wish I was going home meself... You won't be in the back ... you'll be in the passenger seat alongside the driver. Sure, it'll be fine ... "

Other patients tried to mollify Mr. Carroll. In the end he had no choice but to leave by ambulance and the patients and staff tried their best to give him the send-off he deserved. A short while after he'd gone the Matron and Nurse O' Donnell had a whispered discussion just within earshot of the chronic student; the ambulance was not taking Mr. Carroll to his son's home but to a hospice.

THE SIX SEASONS OF THE YEAR

IN ANSWER TO THE TEACHER'S QUESTION, Jimmy Stapleton said there were six seasons in a year. He seemed perplexed that he'd got the answer wrong. He was then invited to name the six seasons for the benefit of the class.

Jimmy took a deep breath. "The conker season, marbles, whipping tops, Cowboys and Indians, tree-climbing and the trolley season."

The teacher was not pleased with the answer. But, Jimmy was right. These were our seasons and they came and went in fairly strict rotation. The timing of some of the seasons was governed by nature. The conker season couldn't start until the chestnuts began to fall from the trees. But there was no reason why marbles made an appearance within a week of St. Patricks' Day. And yet they did without fail.

At the time Jimmy Stapleton gave his answer, the trolley season was upon us and in many ways this was the most challenging season of all because each participant had to make a trolley and then race in it – down a steep hill.

It wasn't that difficult to get the timber, but wheels were like hens' teeth. Kids would scour junk yards, garages and the town dump searching for wheels.

Any wheels would do, but pram wheels were the best. Unfortunately, in the fifties, prams were hardly ever thrown out. Even if mothers had no further use for them they often lent them to younger women or to their daughters. Pram recycling was widespread. It was nothing for thirty children to be raised in one pram – before the springs went.

There were no strollers at the time but go-cars were an early version. These, however, were the sporty version of prams and were even more rare – hens' teeth covered in rocking-horse spit.

During the first week of the trolley season, kids could be seen looking enviously at prams being wheeled along pavements, or parked outside shops. No one was interested in the occupants of the prams, only the wheels. Sometimes Mammies would come out of shops, see us loitering with intent, lusting after wheels – and shoo us away. The few prams that were thrown out that season were quickly pounced on and cannibalised. But no pram wheels came my way.

I did have some luck in the second week of the season. I found a discarded hand truck in the dump. That meant two wheels, and though on the small side, they would do for the back of the wooden orange box I had already collected. I later found a single wheel of a child's tricycle. It was badly rusted but it would do for the front of my trolley which would now of course have to be a three-wheeler. The axles I had already collected were metal rods used to reinforce concrete. As I carried home the wheels I prayed they would fit the axles. They did, though they were a bit loose. That meant the wheels would wobble and reduce the speed of my contraption. It couldn't be helped. Design was limited by what you could get.

On the day of the race we assembled with our trolleys at the top of chosen hill – a long concrete road that led down to the river.

There was one very fancy looking jalopy with wing mirror and cushions. We knew there had been parental involvement in its construction but we kept our thoughts to ourselves. Boys who didn't manage to make trolleys on time would do the pushing at the starting line.

Jimmy Stapleton's trolley had wooden wheels, one of which had already broken. He became a pusher. The last trolley to arrive belonged to Jimmy's older sister, Liz. Her trolley consisted of a coffin lid on bicycle wheels. The Da was an Undertaker. We had never seen anything like it. This contraption was like a greyhound, built for speed.

I was drawn against it in an early heat, and although I got a great push at the starting line, the coffin lid began to nose ahead, and then my front wheel started to wobble so badly that my craft came to an undignified halt.

The coffin lid got through the heats, and in the final it easily beat the fancy trolley. It was so fast it nearly ended up in the river. No one begrudged the winner; it was a breakthrough in technology.

As we dragged our bruised and battered vehicles home we noticed that the chestnut trees were coming into bloom. Of course, Jimmy Stapleton was right. There were six seasons in the year – if not more.

EVERYONE LOSES

WE WERE HOLDING A SEMINAR half-way up the chestnut tree. The subject was the facts of life and it had been triggered by a girl who had just squatted at the foot of the tree, unaware of the sets of eyes that were fixed on her from above. She relieved herself among the conkers we had thrown down, then ran away skipping. Howlin said he knew where babies came from. In retrospect, he was close to the truth, but the rest of us couldn't accept his theory because Mammies just wouldn't do that. One of us thought the navel had some part to play, another, the breasts. The consensus seemed to be that whatever happened – and it probably involved the placing of a hand on the woman's leg above the knee – happened at night when the woman was asleep.

It was a sort of interim conclusion and more research was clearly required to solve the conundrum. Howlin then said loudly, "Ten-a-man...!"

He reminded us about the high stakes game of marbles that was scheduled for later that day. The word had gone round earlier in the week that Slevin and Morrissey were ready to play the long-awaited ten-a-man game. They were a little older than us and were the best marble-players on the street. The idea of each of them risking ten marbles each seemed ridiculous, reckless and even a little mad. But we weren't going to miss it. We left the bough fork of the tree and climbed down. Eager anticipation of the game was in our blood; life could be good at times in that small southern town, though there was no money around and it was nearly always raining.

We assembled at the stretch of footpath that would be closed off for the game. In quiet awe we saw the players place ten marbles each along the diameter of a circle that had just been drawn with white chalk on the flagstone of the footpath. Most games were one-a-man; occasionally there might be a two-a-man game. But ten-a-man was outrageous. It was a fortune in coloured glass and porcelain orbs, which were the coin of our laneway realm. Some of the marbles were treasures, inner-clouded with swirling colours. If one of the players put down a chipped old tawnie, the other player would object, and rightly so. Each player had to put down marbles of equal value – such was the protocol.

Whoever got first shot could clean-up if he kept his head. All marbles knocked out of the circle by his shooter would be his; they would go straight into his pocket. If he got all twenty out, it would mean he would get his own ten back and increase his stock by the other ten, meaning a doubling of his wealth. This was big time, no doubt about it.

Pinking-up was the method used for deciding who would have first shot. Each player would shoot a marble in the direction of the circle to see who could get closest to the twenty 'downers' without touching any of them. If a player actually touched the downers with his shooter during pinking-up then the other automatically got first shot. So you had to get as close as possible without touching. It was like dancing with a girl in a Pioneer Social.

Slevin won the toss and he chose a heavy, pitted ballbearing for pinking up. It was a good choice because the weight of that shooter, combined with its flaws, would give it a purchase on the flagstone and prevent it from sliding, thus increasing the chance of leaving it close to the downers. But, in the event, it didn't serve him well. Charged with adrenaline, no doubt, he overcooked the shot. The ballbearing hit the back wall and ricocheted half-way down the flagstone.

It would be fairly easy for Morrissey to get his shooter nearer to the circle. To improve his chances further he chose a safe route – along a pavement crack, using a patch of lichen to hold the marble to the spot. The strategy worked for him and he won the right of first shot. If he connected well, he could knock a lot of the marbles out of the circle, possibly all of them. No one knew for sure because no one had seen a game of ten-a-man before. We were in uncharted waters.

Morrissey interlaced his fingers, cracked them and shook them loose of imaginary entanglements. Slowly he knelt down at the kerb and selected a big glassy as his shooter.

"Get on with it," Slevin muttered. "And don't pray."

Morrissey gave him a withering look then concentrated on the job in hand. He held the glassy in the crook of his index finger just in front of the thumb. Then he turned his hand to the right until the hand knuckles were resting on the footpath just behind the firing line. His lips began to move.

"He's praying," Slevin announced. Others agreed. Prayer was considered a form of weakness because you were asking God for help. This meant you weren't self-sufficient and couldn't rise to the big occasion. These accusations upset Morrissey, who had to recompose himself. He stood, dusted off his knees, examined his shooting hand and finally knelt again. He set his mouth in a grim straight line. Pressure built up in the thumb which fired the marble. But the shot was nervy and much too fast. The shooter followed a good line but it jumped clear over the twenty downers and didn't even knock one out on the rebound from the wall. Morrissey looked sick with disappointment. His chance of a quick big win was gone.

It was Slevin's turn. He genuflected, anchored his knuckle to the firing line. His glassy had an inner cloud of yellow, like egg yolk, and a blue streak. When it was ejected by his thumb the colours ran together into a blurry green. He knocked six downers clean out of the circle. He began to pick them up as they rolled down the gentle slope of the footpath. But several self-appointed referees simultaneously shouted, "Cuddy knuckle! Cuddy knuckle!" Others nodded sagely. He had pushed his whole hand forward to make the shot, not just the thumb. It was a serious foul.

Slevin protested at first but then he gave a shrug and claimed the cuddy knuckle was unintentional, an accident. But he had to replace all of his winnings on the diameter, bringing the total back up to twenty.

Morrissey took longer than usual to prepare for his turn and he changed his kneeling position several times. The game was just starting in the sense that no marbles had yet been won or lost. We noticed a couple of Teddy Boys over by O'Brien's Garage. They were emigrants returned from England. We remembered them as corner boys before they emigrated. They used to hang around the Tholsel and jeer us on our way to school. They sometimes tried to trip us up if we were running and once or twice we had to avoid gobs of spit. Now here they were back again, though this time with all the trendy gear: slick DAs, long velvet jackets, stovepipe trousers and thick-soled brothel-creepers. They were older than us and, like most returned emigrants, they enjoyed showing us how cool they were and, by implication, how much we were missing out on by not leaving the country. We hoped they wouldn't interfere with the game.

Morrissey was vaguely aware of their presence and this made his initial routines even more jittery and complicated.

"Are you goin' to shoot or not?" Slevin asked in an aggrieved tone of voice, conscious of the fact that he might well have blown his chances with the Cuddy knuckle.

"When I'm ready," Morrissey replied sharply. He looked from his glassy to the downers and back again. Taking aim could be a slow business and he wasn't going to be rushed, especially by his competitor.

"Big game goin' on 'ere or 'wot, mate?" One of the Teds came close to watch.

"Fire, you bugger," the other one said.

Morrissey lost concentration, stood up for a while, went through some more routines and tried to settle himself back down to shoot. We sensed that the interruption did not augur well for the game. We were proved right. One of the Teds, followed by the other, strolled up to the chalk circle and with a couple of kicks from their brothel-creepers sent all the marshalled marbles skittering along the path, veering everywhere at once. Several hit the wall so hard they burst into useless fragments, others sped into the gutter and disappeared down the drain, a few ended up in melted road tar, some were recovered but most were chipped and could never be straight-shooters again. And that was how it came to pass that we never got to see the unprecedented game of ten-a-man.

The following year we were too old to be interested in marbles and by then we had also sorted out the facts of life. There were no more seminars in the chestnut tree.

A CARDIAC AFFAIR

THE SATURDAY-NIGHT HELL would soon begin when the pubs closed. The A and E Unit was girding its loins for the carnage. Nurse Gorman had just come on duty and she decided to deal with the last 'normal' patient before the lunacy began. She asked the patient, Mrs. Boyle, a quiet-spoken woman in her forties, to step into a cubicle and have a seat.

Nurse Gorman noted her particulars on the standard form and took her vital signs. Mrs. Boyle was a pleasant woman with two daughters, one of whom suffered from Down's syndrome. She answered all of the questions fully and without demurring. Nurse Gorman had to inform her that although they wouldn't turn her away, they were not obliged to treat her since this was an A and E facility. She should have gone to her own GP in the first instance.

"Oh, I know, Nurse, and I'm sorry. But I think it might be my heart. You can't take chances when it's the heart."

Nurse Gorman looked at her notes again. She didn't think there was anything wrong with the woman's heart but it wasn't her call. "If you stay here, I'll have a doctor examine you in a few minutes." Nurse Gorman wasn't paid enough to bypass procedures.

Mrs. Boyle sat in the cubicle, which had drapes like her shower curtains – blue dolphins on a white background with occasional green curves and yellow starfish to indicate the sea. She flicked mindlessly through a woman's magazine while she waited. The numerous glossy stills of leggy, made-up models and stars did not suggest to her that any great strides had been made by the feminist movement over the last thirty years.

Dr Jameson swooped in like a seagull landing on water. He reviewed the history and vital signs, asked about her symptoms and listened to her heart. Her pulse and blood pressure were perfectly normal and her heart sounded fine.

"Do you have that pins and needles feeling right now?" he asked.

"No, Doctor. Not at the moment."

"And you're not on any medication?"

"No. Maybe an Aspro every now and again for a headache. But that's all."

Dr Jameson replaced the stethoscope around his neck and straightened up. "I don't think there's anything wrong with your heart, Mrs. Boyle."

"I wonder … maybe a stress test … to rule out ischaemia…?"

"I don't think that is necessary." Dr Jameson sometimes wondered if the internet had been invented to complicate his life. With all the medical websites around why did anyone bother consulting a doctor at all? When the internet developed into a global brain wouldn't it make everyone redundant, especially diagnosticians?

"Well, I…"

"If you have any more worries in the future you should discuss them with your GP. If he thinks further investigation is needed, he will send you to a consultant. OK? Good." He started to hustle and bustle as if he had turned into a cyclone; his body language was loud and clear in dismissing her.

Mrs. Boyle left the A and E Unit just as the first drunks began to stagger in, shouting obscenities. At least they were already anaesthetised. She took the bus home, hoping that her husband, Danny, had started the tea for their two daughters. She loved the way her older daughter, Sally, looked after her handicapped sister, Bernadette. The innocence of both of them warmed her heart.

When tea was over Mrs Boyle helped her daughters with their homework, bemoaning the fact that Bernadette's homework would probably be too complicated for her next year. She already had her foot to the floor and was finding it hard to keep up. She really needed a special teacher but there were none available. The government had cut back on health spending and had absolutely no idea how the cuts affected people like the Boyles. Her husband, Danny, had to work a double shift; he didn't complain about it but she knew he couldn't physically do any more. Their social life was nonexistent. When they first got married they went out twice a week, usually with friends. Now they didn't go out at all. Since he was the more sociable of the two it probably affected him more, though he never complained about it.

A week later Mrs. Boyle presented again at the A and E, complaining of chest pain. The usual protocols were followed, Nurse Gorman taking the history and vital signs and Dr. Jameson listening to her heart.

"I really don't think there's anything wrong with your heart, Mrs. Boyle. It could be indigestion."

"Oh, I never get that. Is the blood pressure all right?"

"Perfect. But that wouldn't cause pain in any case. Not in the chest … or anywhere else for that matter. It's asymptomatic."

"You're quite busy tonight," Mrs. Boyle observed, buttoning up her blouse.

"Yes, for a Thursday night. "Dr Jameson prepared to sweep out of the cubicle. This one had swordfish and fiddler crabs on the curtains.

"I suppose it's better in here than out…"

"I don't follow." Even when he hesitated, he managed to give the impression of bustling. He seemed to strain against some hidden entanglement that anchored him to the spot.

"Safer … it's safer in here."

Dr Jameson sat back down on the kick-stool and looked hard at her. "Safer? You feel safer … sort of reassured … in here?"

"Well, yes … I mean with all the nurses and

doctors … professional people…"

"Carers," he prompted.

"Yes." She forced a laugh. "People trained to care."

"In white coats?"

"Well, that's part of it I suppose. I mean if you don't feel safe in a hospital where can you feel safe?"

"I see. I see… Well, your heart is fine, Mrs. Boyle. Don't worry about it." Dr Jameson watched her as she left the Unit. She paused at the water fountain and looked around as if reluctant to leave. Before closing her file Dr Jameson wrote 'M.S?', then, with a flourish, added another question mark. He put the retractable pen in the top pocket of his white coat.

The next time she appeared he had to make a special, though not quite successful, effort to remain polite. He asked if she had gone to her GP who, he pointed out, was supposed to provide primary care.

"Oh, it's not me this time, Doctor. It's my daughter Sally." She pushed forward a shy ten-year-old with long fair hair. He spoke to the child, asked about her symptoms and did some preliminary tests. She had been throwing up and did look wan.

"It's probably just something she ate," Dr Jameson said.

Mrs. Boyle told him in an aside that she thought there had been blood in the vomit. Dr

Jameson decided to keep the child overnight for observation. Mrs. Boyle offered to stay in the hospital with her.

"There's no need for that."

"I don't mind. I won't be in the way. I've brought my toothbrush," she added with a slight attempt at levity.

"It's not possible, I'm afraid." He admitted Sally and brusquely walked her mother to the door. When she left, he had a word with one of the ward nurses.

The next morning, he checked on Sally. She had thrown up two more times during the early part of the night and then slept fairly well. There was no blood in evidence and analysis showed that the vomit contained baking soda and salt. Dr Jameson discharged her and sent her home in the front seat of an ambulance.

He asked Nurse Gorman to get him Mrs. Boyle's file and asked her to stay while he riffled through it. He noticed that Mrs. Boyle had presented a couple of other times before he had joined the hospital and she had been sent home each time.

"Do you know what we have here, Nurse Gorman?"

"No, Doctor."

"M.S. full blown."

"Multiple Scler…?"

"No. No. Munchausen's Syndrome. Just as I suspected. And now it's developed into the proxy form."

"I don't follow."

"She likes being around nurses and doctors. So, at first, she herself feigned symptoms. But now she's using someone else, her daughter. That's the proxy form."

"Oh, hospital pests. I've heard of them. But I never came across any."

"Well now you have. The next time she presents, get rid of her. I'll tell my colleagues. You should tell yours." He wrote on the file that his earlier suspicion of Munchausen's had now been confirmed. In addition, Mrs. Boyle had deliberately caused illness in her daughter and thereby displayed classic symptoms of Munchausen's by proxy. There was nothing whatsoever wrong with Mrs. Boyle's heart. Hard-pressed medical staff should be alerted to the situation; considerable resources had already been wasted.

In the weeks following Mrs. Boyle made a couple of visits to the A and E Unit and was sent home without examination. She was advised to consult with her GP with a view to getting a referral to a psychotherapist.

On a faintly sunny day in the middle of Autumn, Mrs. Boyle's husband, Danny, rang the family GP who responded as quickly as he could.

Danny met him on the doorstep and said, "I think you're too late, Doctor."

The GP took the stairs two steps at a time and found Mrs. Boyle in bed. There was no movement and no pulse. She held a framed photo of her daughters in her cold hands.

At least he had been aware that she was running out of time, but they had not told the children.

Two days after the funeral a lawyer rang Danny and asked to meet him in the lobby of the Dunphy Hotel. When they met, Danny recognised him because he had seen him on a couple of occasions with his wife. The lawyer had a copy of the death certificate on the table in front of him. Left ventricular Hypertrophy, followed by heart failure. The lawyer told him that Mrs. Boyle had instructed him to sue Dr. Jameson for medical negligence. On several occasions he had failed to diagnose his wife's illness, then turned her away from the hospital on the grounds of a false diagnosis of Munchausen's Syndrome. The lawyer said that, on the basis of the facts presented, it was an open-and-shut case. He told Danny to start thinking about numbers and not to worry about anything. All medical consultants carried hefty insurance, partly subsidised by the State. Law-suits such as this one helped keep doctors on their feet and reduced the level of arrogance that tended to go with the medical profession. He suggested a follow-up meeting.

When Danny got home he began the task of throwing out his wife's various medicines; she had doubled the doses to help mask her symptoms when she visited the A and E Unit. Then he went into the children's bedroom, kissed them on their foreheads, and began to read them a story.

THE AUCTION

TIM ARMSTRONG WAS HAPPY where he was but his wife wanted a bigger house. A pillow under his head at night, and a roof over it, was all Tim wanted or so he said on more than one occasion to his wife. Until he stopped saying it and he began to see the issue more clearly through her eyes. Anyway, the family was expanding and it seemed a reasonable time to trade up.

Many weekends were devoted to looking at houses and knocking on the walls, a habit he'd picked up from the surveyor they'd used to check out their existing abode. He could tell the difference between a stud partition and a block wall, but that was about it.

For many people, looking at houses was a lifelong hobby, and Tim sometimes met friends and colleagues in the toilets or basements of different properties on view. The initial embarrassment of making smalltalk over a duck-egg-blue bidet or discoloured Victorian W.C. gradually faded away as he became a more experienced house-hunter.

He had to listen to the feverish patois of different estate agents, exchange cards, and hope fervently never to meet them again. The suffering came to an end eventually when they found a house they both liked and the location – near a river – was a bonus. It would be sold by auction and the estate agent, whom Tim had already christened 'Biggs' after the great train robber, answered one of their questions with an insouciance calculated to indicate that it was a sellers' market, "We're guiding it in the late 150s."

"But what do you think it will fetch?" Tim asked.

Biggs ignored the question and repeated word for word the ghastly jargon with which he had just assaulted him.

Another estate agent had assessed Tim's house as, "Somewhere in the approximate vicinity of the early 90s."

Tim assumed that this probably referred to price rather than space-time coordinates and, by subtracting these fuzzy estimates came up with an even fuzzier figure which he presented to his bank manager who in turn gave approval in principle for a most complex endowment mortgage with tracker features and a bullet pay-off. Did anyone really understand mortgages, Tim wondered, especially the ones that came with bells and whistles? He knew he was going to be ripped off by the bank as he had been in the past, and by the estate agents and lawyers. Everyone had their hands out for fees or brown envelopes. Changing houses was like putting a bloodied limb into a shark-infested sea. This indeed was one of the reasons Tim would have been happy to have stayed in his own humble abode. The dice were heavily loaded against any form of change in this strange, conservative, sheltered society.

On the morning of the auction, Biggs phoned Tim and offered to do the bidding for him. Tim demurred, having a vision of figures rapidly mounting up on a fee-o-meter, but Biggs insisted, saying that there were some tricks of the trade that could save 'an ordinary punter big bucks'.

Later that morning, Biggs rang from his Mercedes to ask Tim if he had done his numbers.

"I'm going to bailout at 165,000 Euros. That's the absolute maximum."

"165 grand. Got ya."

Inside the auction rooms, Tim kicked his heels for a while, watching people drift into the hall where the business would be done. He tried to assess the competition but failed. The whole idea of an auction was anathema to him; it was far too competitive for his taste – to the point of aggression.

He spotted Biggs standing in an office and went to fetch him for the big event. He didn't mean to eavesdrop, but through the half-open door he couldn't help but hear Biggs say to the auctioneer, "My guy's going to 165, but I think you could get him up to 175. Same signals as before, OK? Fine."

Tim had heard about collusion but this was extreme. Biggs was supposed to be acting for him and there he was, selling him out. He felt nauseous and wondered if he shouldn't just walk away from it all. No, he decided to see it through, but under no circumstances would he let Biggs go one penny above 165. If he tried it, Tim would stand up, disown the bid and walk out.

The vendor's auctioneer stood behind a podium and Tim and Biggs sat together at the end of the sixth row. The hall was now quite full and there was an air of expectancy not unlike that in a theatre before the curtain rises. Tim had forgotten how tense and intimidating it could be – even before the bidding started.

The auctioneer started his spiel about the house, a wonderful family home treated with loving care, a large south-facing well-stocked garden, not overlooked, wide frontage, river views etc. Then he inquired if there were any questions interested parties wanted to ask before the bidding got under way. The firm's solicitor was there to answer any legal questions.

A well-heeled woman raised her hand and said she had a minor question in relation to the curtilage of the property. The auctioneer invited her up to the front of the room where a whispered conference took place. As Tim watched this performance his bile rose for a second time that morning, and nerves were already playing havoc with his stomach. The whispering was designed to leave other bidders in the dark; it was *caveat emptor* to the Nth degree. Transparency was clearly a luxury the seller and fee-mongers could not afford. The woman returned to her seat, apparently reassured by whatever the solicitor had told her.

The auctioneer looked keenly around the room. He was about to ask for an opening bid when he was interrupted by a voice from the back of the hall.

"I have some questions." Many heads turned to see an elegantly turned out man who had just entered through the double doors. "I represent a client in London. He is interested in this property but has concerns about flooding when the river bursts its banks. A survey revealed structural cracks and an infestation in the roof timbers…"

"Please, please…! Could you come up here?" The auctioneer belatedly found his voice and made abrupt beckoning gestures. The elegant man had the whispered conference with the auctioneer and the vendor's solicitor. He shook his head several times and eventually bade them adieu, saying that his client would no longer be interested in the property. He walked down the centre aisle and straight out the door.

The auctioneer was clearly upset but tried manfully to recover his composure. He debunked the very thought of flooding and began to rhapsodise about the house again. He then asked for an opening bid of 120 thousand. There was a long silence and he was about to begin another eulogy when a bid of 75 thousand was made. The auctioneer pleaded for realism. The bids crawled upwards and after half an hour the figure had only reached 120 thousand. The auctioneer looked down at Biggs and announced that he would suspend the proceedings for a few minutes to confer with the vendor.

When he returned he said that the property was not yet on the market and he requested more bids which should reflect more accurately 'the inherent value of this imposing house'.

Biggs entered the fray and, competing with three others, nudged the price up to 130 thousand at which point the house was 'on the market'. This announcement did not produce the expected frisson and only a few more bids were made, despite the exhortations of the auctioneer and a few desperate glances towards Biggs. A telephone bid – possibly a phantom one – shifted the price up a notch.

Eventually the house was knocked down, reluctantly and with a poor grace, to Tim at a price of 140 thousand, which was well below his reserve and even further below the figure the colluding agents were hoping to extract from him. The latter could barely conceal their disappointment as Tim signed the deposit cheque. The seller, who had obviously been promised a better price, wore a very pained expression, and referred to that "fucking ponce from London who had thrown a spanner in the works."

A short time later Tim got rid of Biggs, who stayed behind with the auctioneer, and went out to the street. It was such a relief to be away from the cloying, faintly corrupt atmosphere of the auction room. The faint breeze that came from the river refreshed him; it was like a blessing. He went into a nearby pub for a celebratory pint. Then he ordered a second as the elegant man joined him at the bar and slapped him on the back.

EXCELLENT BUT NOT NATURAL

MONICA KEOGH had been complaining to her neighbour, Sheila, that her husband didn't seem to listen to her anymore, but used her as a sounding board for his own ideas, most of which – the implication went – weren't his at all but ones which he had probably filched from his work colleagues.

Sheila gave the age-old advice. Talk to him about it. Sit down together and talk it out. She, herself, had had to do that with her husband, Cyril, on more than one occasion.

"But he doesn't listen." Monica began to wonder whether her best friend, Sheila, listened. Maybe nobody really listened; was it possible that everyone lived in soundproof cocoons in splendid isolation, and could not communicate at all?

Sheila corrected her gaffe. "No, I mean *sit him down. Arrange it so that he has to listen.*" After some discussion of the logistics, Monica thought it was worth a shot.

That evening when Bob got home she sat him down with a cup of tea and gently took his newspaper away from him. When his eyes started to roam in the direction of the TV, she switched off the set. She had considerately checked the TV listings in advance; there was no football on. Then he looked at his watch as if he were late and should be some place else at that moment, a sort of alibi in advance.

"I want to say something and you're not listening."

"I am," he said vacantly, his eyes still swivelling about in search of distractions, a crack in the ceiling, a fly on the wall.

"Not really." Just then the Angelus bell sounded and Bob crossed himself and went into prayerful mode. Monica watched him helplessly, not daring to interrupt a prayer. Was he communicating with God – a nonexistent being in her book – or merely going through the motions? When he began to look around for the newspaper in the middle of the prayer, she gave up and went out to the kitchen, from where, after a while, she could hear the muffled sounds of the TV drifting from the sitting room. The marriage was virtually over. She had to decide whether to drive a stake through its heart or not. She couldn't understand how Bob, and apparently other men, could be happy in a marriage where there was no real communication whatever. What did they get from such a relationship? A regular supply of sex and food? Was that it? Of course, the automatic satisfaction of both those needs meant that they didn't have to go hunting anymore. Obviously when men were hunters they had to communicate; their lives depended on it. But now…? Hmmmnnnn.

The weekend came and went. She did the shopping, he played golf on both days – following a ball for miles was clearly a surrogate for hunting. They passed each other quietly in the house; there was no acrimony, only silence.

Then on Tuesday evening an extraordinary thing happened. When Bob came home from work, he sat Monica down and brought her a cup of tea.

"I'm sorry about the other day," he said, "What was it you wanted to say?" He brought over a chair and sat down opposite her, an expression of intense concentration on his face.

At first, she thought it was some kind of trick, but after a while she could tell that he was serious. Now that she had his attention, she found it hard to begin; she even thought that she was being patronised, though she quickly realised that that was not his style. It was like being on stage, but gradually she hit her stride. When she mentioned that he was a poor listener he didn't disagree or turn away, but actually nodded.

"You heard what I said?" She needed confirmation.

"Yes. Absolutely." He nodded slowly, affirming the truth to himself, metabolising it.

She went on to explain how on occasion he could be quite rude, possibly without realising it, by interrupting her and changing the subject, thus trivialising her concerns.

"I see."

"Do you? Do you really see how that makes me feel?"

"Maybe not fully…" A stirring movement of his hand, as if he were slowly whisking cream, urged her to go on. His face wore a furrowed look of concern.

"What?"

"Interrupting … how it makes you…"

"Yes… feel …"

"Not good."

"No." She checked his body language again. Whether it was his facial expression or postural echo he definitely seemed to be tuned into the right wavelength for once. "Irritated … actually, worse than that. Hurt, very hurt. As if my views don't matter at all … as if I'm not capable of having views of my own…"

"Not capable… Oh Lord…" He screwed his face up in self-loathing.

"Yes, exactly." The tea he'd made was too strong but now wasn't the time to quibble. "And you never let me finish a joke or a story in company. You have to dive in with the punchline. It's almost as if you don't trust me to get it right, that you're afraid … I might embarrass you."

"Embarrass?"

"Yes. Can you imagine how that feels?"

"Sort of…" His eyebrows came together in an arch in puzzlement and worry.

She went on to explain how it felt to be second fiddle all the time. She felt amorphous, inconsequential, not rooted in the world. "It's a terrible feeling."

"Mmmm, mmmm. Go on."

"And the worst part is…" She hesitated. Emotion choked her for a while.

"The worst part…?" He gently prompted.

"My father used to make me feel like that," she blurted out, on the verge of tears.

"Your father…?"

"Yes. I always had the impression that he wanted a son. I wasn't really to be trusted in a man's world. I wasn't any good at sports, though, God, I tried to be. But nothing I did was good enough. There was no way I could please him. There was always the sense that I was letting the side down, embarrassing him… Love was conditional. It had to be earned. No matter what I did I had no way of earning it…"

"That must've been … you know … really…"

"Awful. Yes. Your best is never good enough. You can't compete. You're not even in the game." She drew a small handkerchief from the sleeve of her cardigan and blew her nose. He sat there shaking his head sympathetically.

"So, you thought that I…"

"Yes. You continued the pattern, probably without realising it. You didn't listen. Finished my sentences for me. What else was I to think?"

He asked her how she felt about it. His eyes were opened so wide that the lids were squashed against the sockets. The movement of scalp over skull caused a slight shift in the position of his ears.

"Unwanted … unloved." She sniffled for a while then pulled herself together and continued. "Feeling patronised too. Oh, I hate being patronised. You've no idea how I hate that."

"Being patronised… mmmmm… it must be…"

"Absolutely. It kills me. It brings up all those old feelings of inadequacy…" Monica continued at length and finally talked herself out. Bob never wavered in his concentration and followed every word she uttered, and every nuance of every word. She felt better than she had in a long while; her partner was miraculously restored to her. She thanked him for his conversion and his understanding.

The next morning, she gave him a cooked breakfast in bed and a big sloppy kiss. Later in the day she met Sheila in the shopping mall and both women went for a coffee. Excitedly, Monica described the transformation that had occurred and said she wanted to set the record straight. She had been too critical of Bob and now felt guilty about it. She described how wonderful he had been, how he hadn't just listened, but had prompted her to continue when she faltered.

"Oh," Sheila said, "It must be that staff appraisal course they're on."

"What?"

"At work. Cyril is on the same course. It's about how to listen to staff. Rogerian listening therapy, I think he called it. They were told to try it out at home to see how it worked… What's the matter? Monica, what's up?"

When Bob got home from work, he threw his scuffed leather briefcase on the hall stand and went into the kitchen where he gave Monica a peck on the cheek. It occurred to him how much better he knew her now after his application of Rogerian listening therapy. The damn thing worked!

"I had a very bad day," she said.

"A bad day… Mmmmm, mmmmm. Tell me about it… Ummmm, go on…" He sat opposite her and although his eyes were fixed on her face, or maybe because of it, he didn't see the sweep of her arm. But he did feel the force of the hand which caught him on the side of the head.

GRASPING AIR

IF YOU HAD ASKED LUCINDA ten years ago if she would ever make a living out of hugging, she'd have laughed in your face. And yet, here she was, at the door of her comfortable four-bedroomed 'House of Hugs', collecting groceries she'd ordered online. The van driver was a fresh-faced young man who reminded her of her son, Robbie, who had gone for a walk one day in the summer of 2016 with a laptop in his rucksack, and never come back.

Lucinda had gone through the agonies of uncertainty and then grief – on her own at first, but that proved too much so she found herself in therapy, where she formed a strong bond of friendship with Malcolm Fernet, whose partner had taken an overdose of sleeping pills. The two bereft people now lived together as friends in the comfortable house on Loch Raven Drive. Hugging had been part of the therapy they had received, and for some years now, they provided a hugging service for anyone in need. 'Hug don't Lug', became one of their slogans. People in mental anguish could relate only to the simplest slogans, which they often repeated like mantras or incantations. It was amazing how many people lugged problems around with them instead of hugging them out.

They didn't charge fees, but clients – they preferred to call them 'beneficiaries' – could leave a donation. No one would be turned away for lack of money. Lucinda and Malcolm made a good living and were quite surprised by this. It didn't require much skill or training to give good hugs and yet not many people had entered that profession for which there was a surprising demand. The huggers benefited too; there was something curative about the mutual embrace of fellow human beings. It was the equivalent of monkey-grooming or the calming effect that older bull elephants often had on troubled young males, especially at mating time.

Verbal counselling had never delivered the goods and now the emphasis was switching to nonverbal support. There was also a trend away from Californian exotica, such as rebirth, chakras, and Native American drumming in the woods, and back to more simple touch therapy. Was it a fad or did it meet some deep need? Lucinda and Malcolm didn't know the answer to that question, but it didn't worry them unduly.

Did hugging ever slide into sex? Sometimes a beneficiary would make moves in that direction but Lucinda and Malcolm could read the signs early on and diplomatically disengage. Once, Malcolm had to rush into the hugging 'clinic' to pull someone off Lucinda, but that was the exception. On another occasion an entire stag party arrived on the assumption that the place was a brothel. But in general, beneficiaries would accept what was written on the tin; a hug was a hug. It wasn't a massage with a 'happy ending'. And there were almost always good results after the first session, which usually involved a lot of weeping. Tissues were often not enough to cope with convulsive weeping, which could sometimes be uncannily like retching. So, both therapists kept large towels within easy reach to deal with the liquid detritus of past unhappy lives. Occasionally two or three further sessions were advised but rarely more than that. Unlike conventional therapists, they didn't keep clients on a string for years.

Lucinda was a better hugger than Malcolm. Her hugs were warmer and more natural and she often ran her hand instinctively up and down the back of the beneficiary. This became known as the 'hug 'n rub' technique. The rub provided additional reassurance and, like the proverbial pat on the back – a gesture that spoke in a universal language – it vouched for the person's likeability. These techniques didn't come naturally to Malcolm, but he worked hard until he perfected them. They were never as organic as those employed by Lucinda, but he worked hard at them.

Lucinda and Malcolm were having breakfast in the dining room which was decorated in earth tones – saffron carpet, mustard drapes with Indian red tiebacks, ethnic throw-rugs on wooden floors. Smells of perfumed candles – the only Californian bric-à-brac they allowed – drifted in from the hallway.

"I had a beneficiary last evening," Lucinda

began, "who had a lot of drink on board."

"He didn't try anything on?" Malcom asked.

"Well, not really. Nothing sexual. But he wanted to wrestle…"

"Wrestle?"

"He kept on muttering about how Jacob wrestled all night with the Archangel Gabriel. I'm not sure we should deal with someone in their cups."

"I agree. The alcohol screens out the reality of what's happening. So the therapeutic effect is watered down, if not lost." Malcolm had to deal with a coke fiend some months ago. It was just impossible to bring him back. He asked him to return when he was clean but he never saw him again.

"I think we should write that into our promotional literature." Lucinda carefully cut the crust off a slice of toast and slid it on to Malcom's plate. He liked crusts, especially with a smear of marmalade.

"OK, I'll drop into the printer's today. It's a quick fix. I can tweak the website myself."

"I often think that ordinary reality isn't enough for young people today. I don't know what's gone wrong exactly but they seem to want a different mode of existence. I remember once when the hugging was over I brought the beneficiary into the garden. She had never seen thistledown before. She cried and cried, as she watched the white spores fly around. She had seen far more impressive things in 3D wraparound movies like 'Avatar', but the simple thistledown got to her."

Malcolm nodded. "In my day we played with a ball in the street and enjoyed ourselves. Now it's … it's not enough for kids. Maybe the internet has opened too many doors… I don't know."

"Mmnn," Lucinda mulled it over. "Jacob wrestling the Angel. At least it was hands-on, wasn't it? There was almost personal contact with God. He wasn't so far distant. But then when Moses went up the mountain, God had become more mystical, less personal… And what did the Israelites do? They created a golden calf. Even though it wasn't alive, they could see it and touch it…"

Malcolm nodded. "They could hug it."

"Yes, they could."

———————

In a small room in the North Western quadrant of the city Ruben lay on a narrow bed, his head encased in a Virtual Reality Helmet (VRH) with built-in headphones and versatile touch pad; it was immersive and virus-protected, all in all a drool-worthy rig. His senses were focused on driving a flying car over a winning line etched on the sky. He was excited because he was close to beating his own record. On a small side screen he could see that his pulse was elevated. Unfortunately, in the final moments he encountered random air turbulence; he tried to steer above it but that lengthened the course. He failed to equal his own record by a tenth of a second.

It was 3.30 in the morning; he'd been playing for twenty-three hours straight and hadn't eaten. It was too late to eat now, so he went to bed with the VRH and control unit in their respective pouches. He liked to sleep with them. But it was also convenient to keep them close because there was every possibility he would want to play something when he woke in the morning. Indeed, if he woke during the night he could go for a walk on Pluto or some other planet. As a child he had liked the dawn chorus and murmurations of starlings, but they were very rare occurrences and he had to wait for long periods. With the help of technology he didn't have to leave his room or wait more than a second to tune in to these frequencies.

As it happened, he dreamt about Rebecca – the first and only girl he had gone out with. It was a lucid dream and he could see her brown curly hair and hear her laughter, especially the high notes. He could feel her breath on his face. He couldn't remember what triggered her laughter. Had he been a good joke-teller? She was into gaming too. Once, when she came back with him to his room he persuaded her to shed her clothes and he followed suit. All seemed to be going according to plan, but then for no apparent reason she became tense and started to panic. He remembered her screams and was dumbfounded by them. This was not the way it happened on porn sites. Why on earth would she protest?

But Ruben wasn't too disappointed. He had to admit that her body was far from perfect; there were freckles, blotches and hairs that he never expected, and she wasn't all smooth depilated curves; there were bumps and knots here and there. Even at her relatively young age there were signs of incipient cellulite. She didn't really measure up to his favourite online women, who were airbrushed to perfection. Truth be told, Rebecca wasn't in any danger because he had not become tumescent – though he did as soon as he got back to his helmet and entered a decent program that met his every interactive whim.

One day in late spring, Ruben experienced a dizzy spell while he was sorting through a selection of programs. He put it to the back of his mind, entered the VRH and walked through the Serengeti for the next couple of days in the company of rogue elephants and rutting lions. When he exited that tour and was about to embark for Alpha Centauri, the dizziness came on again and he decided he would have to see about it – after another two or three tours.

The doctor didn't have to run too many tests; he had encountered this syndrome before. He visualised the pathology as a bag of psychic toxins that had built up during years of pubescent escapism. His own father had made him take the pledge when he received the sacrament of confirmation. The promise not to drink until the age of twenty-one was an inspired commitment because it meant that the teenager had to encounter and get through all the anxieties of growing up, on his own without the crutch of alcohol. He spoke to Ruben for a while but could see that his words were not getting through. Ruben fidgeted with his VRH all through the session. The doctor gave him a card for the House of Hugs and made Ruben promise that he would attend.

It was only because the dizzy spells got worse and became more frequent that Ruben did turn up at the House of Hugs one evening when a light snow lay on the ground. Lucinda gave a preliminary spiel during which Ruben began to fidget. Lucinda observed his growing nervousness and the fact that several times he reached out to touch his pouched VRH. The thought occurred that this young man was about the same age as her son would be – assuming he was still alive. For all she knew, he might very well be her son. She had always had the intuition that Robbie had not gone far away, that he would have stayed close enough to her, just as this young man valued proximity to the VRH. It was a security thing, like apron strings. At any rate, she was convinced that the empathy she felt would potentiate the therapy.

She slowly opened her arms and moved closer to him on the specially modified couch. Her left hand had just reached his right shoulder when he went into a crouch and began to moan. Instinctively, she moved closer and his moans turned into wails and indicated that he was approaching hysteria. She had rarely encountered such fear before. She buzzed for Malcolm, who entered almost immediately.

"I don't think he's ready," Malcolm said, noting the foetal posture of the beneficiary. "He's been too long in the wilderness."

"You're right," Lucinda replied reluctantly. It was so sad, but he wasn't real anymore. Not only that but he didn't want to be real; in fact he dreaded it. There was no way back. She began to weep. So many young people, including her son and Malcolm's partner, had nothing to hold onto and were sliding off the face of the earth. She assured Ruben over and over again that she would not hug him. Eventually his wailing tailed away and he looked up with craven relief in his eyes. She handed him his VRH, into which he immediately, and with gratitude, encased his head.

HUMILIATION TV

BARB, THE PRODUCER OF 'TORPEY TIME', was becoming more anxious about the show as the months passed. Her husband, Matthew Torpey, who presented the show, was becoming too relaxed, cavalier even. She could remember the early days when he clutched with stagefright and when he went over the script notes repeatedly like a man possessed. Back then when he went on set he was like a tightly strung tennis racket, smashing back balls with amazing speed. Now there was a kind of slack world-weariness, verging on cynicism.

Matt was happy to wing it. His wit had grown flabby; he was content to use autocue and script cards that he referred to in full view of the cameras. What saved him was that he was a big name, almost a national treasure. But it was unprofessional, and Barb often wondered if audiences would continue to indulge him, and if so, for how long.

Tonight's show was pretty standard fare. Matt dozed off in Make-Up while getting his grey spots darkened. Barb pulled up a chair beside him and woke him up to go over the running order once more.

"That's OK, Barbs," Matt said. "No need to fuss. It's the usual formula." To the make-up girl he said, "She's like a mother hen."

Barb passed a hand through her brown hair

and wondered if and when her lazy darling husband might hit white water. Like bankruptcy, it could happen in two ways: gradually or suddenly. They had both ridden the crest of the New Wave, what some TV critics now dubbed 'The Horse Shoot', after the movie 'They Shoot Horses, Don't They?' Viewers seemed to like watching other people being humiliated whether the economy was in recession or not. She could never understand why so many people would go on air voluntarily, knowing what lay in store. Was it a modern human need to have fifteen minutes of fame regardless of personal cost? Was it due to poor education or some lack of self-awareness? Did it matter as long as the ratings remained solid? From the producer's point of view, there was no percentage in looking a gift horse in the mouth.

An intern passed by, announcing, "Fifteen minutes to go."

"Did you hear that, Matt?" Barb thought it advisable to check.

"Yes, don't fret, Honey. I'm ready as I'll ever be."

It was Barb's job to worry, and she now, once again, confronted her other abiding concern: the risk of a lawsuit. It was always possible, she thought, that after a night of hectic feverishness in the studio, a guest would wake up the next morning and in the cold light of dawn realise how cruelly they had been exposed. What if they decided to end it all? And what if relatives sought redress from Matt and the TV Station. They were insured of course, but it could be the end of their careers.

But it hadn't happened yet. No suicides, no writs. It seemed as if the guests just didn't mind *how* they came across on TV as long as they appeared on the damn thing. The more immediate concern was that Matt would become too laid back and fall over. Falling in any shape or form was not something the American public could tolerate.

Matt cupped a hand to his ear. "Ah, my public are arriving."

Barb, too, could hear the sounds of the studio audience, murmuring and shuffling between the raked rows. They were usually well behaved though prone to a little pushing and shoving to get the best seats, those which were closest to the cameras. It was as if they too hoped for a brief exposure to the wider world. TV cameras had some magical properties she couldn't fully understand. She looked through a chink in the curtain to see the phenomenon that had always intrigued her: how the dead space of the studio suddenly became alive. It was like an infusion of blood into an atrophied muscle. She was a good judge of audiences and this seemed to be a good one, i.e., one that was willing to suspend disbelief at the drop of a surrealistic bowler hat. As Matt became lazier his audiences miraculously seemed to become dumber – which was just as well. It was of course possible that causality ran the other way.

She finished her coffee and went out to tell the audience about some housekeeping matters, like exits and mobile phones. She used to hire a warm-up man, but Matt insisted they didn't need one now, the implication being that his charisma and A List status were enough. But Barb made a few quips anyway and had a couple of amusing interactions with members of the band to get everyone in the right mood. She told the happily captive audience they had a good show lined up for them as if they were the chosen few, and not the five to six million viewers out there in the ether.

At a signal from the Stage Manager she introduced Matt, who received a noisy reception when he entered through the deep blue drapes, with hands joined, giving his trademark Chinese bow.

There was nothing special about the show. The formula behind it was tried and tested and had proved itself fit for purpose. The first guest was an elderly white woman who was dismayed by the fact that all of her six daughters were lesbians who would give her no grandchildren. Her oldest daughter sat beside her dressed in boots, jeans and a lumberjack jacket. The discussion ranged far and wide, from lifestyle choices to surrogacy, from IVF to gay marriage.

"Well," Matt cooed, "I guess it's all part of life's rich tapestry."

A man in the audience said he had a question.

"Can I ask the daughter if she, I mean … did she inter … encourage her younger sisters to become lesbians?"

"That's outrageous," the daughter said aggressively. "Shut your mouth."

Matt supported her. "I can't allow that question. If all of the sisters were hetero you wouldn't ask that." He began his wind-up of that section. The audience did not question his decision.

During the ad break he sat with Barb, who seemed pleased enough.

"Being PC at last," she ribbed him. There were a few times at the start of his career when he had to apologise for making inappropriate remarks.

"Oh, she probably fiddled with her siblings," Matt said, "But I've no intention of being crucified by the LGBT crowd."

"And they said you'd never learn." Barb gave a broad grin. A decade ago he might have fanned the flames, but not now. National treasures like he was now were part of the establishment and knew which side their bread was buttered on. Donald Trump was the only sleazebag who could air his true views in public and get away with it. Besides, Matt just didn't want the hassle of controversy; it required a lot of psychic energy.

In the yellowing light of an overstuffed lounge in New Jersey, a heavy-set, blue-visaged man watched the programme with growing annoyance, which he directed at his long-suffering wife.

"He wouldn't allow that question," he grumbled. "Who the hell does he think he is?"

"He's..." his wife was about to explain who Matt Torpey was, but her husband silenced her with a hand. The second part of the show was commencing and he leant forward in anticipation of having his senses assaulted again by that Torpey asshole. This time it would be personal.

———————————

Matt introduced his next guest, Maria, who was heavily with child. Her partner, Fabio, did not believe he was the father.

"Why do you not trust her..." Matt checked his card, "...Fabio?"

"She go out a lot," Fabio said.

"Well that's hardly evidence," Matt put in. "I go out a lot too and I..."

The studio audience thought this was hilarious and began to laugh and chant, "Matt, Matt, Matt; we smell a rat, rat, rat!"

After much argy-bargy the usual doctor was

brought on to give a thumbnail sketch of the importance of trust in relationships. Then, to hushes, he opened the envelope which contained the results of a prenatal noninvasive paternity test. In a slow, deliberate voice he announced that Fabio was right to doubt his paternity because the child Maria was carrying was not his. Fabio launched a triumphant fist into the air and his unfaithful wife ran off the stage in tears. Matt followed her out and a camera crew followed him.

"Come back in," he urged her. "We can fix this ... all the counselling you need at our expense."

Slowly, Maria's tears dried and reluctantly she returned to the set where Fabio swore that he'd leave her because she was a promiscuous bitch.

But then Matt produced a surprise guest, a burly young man bursting out of a flimsy black tank-top. It turned out that he was Fabio's secret lover. All hell broke loose. Maria took off her shoes, threw one at Fabio and the other at the gay partner. The security men stepped in.

"Matt, Matt, Matt; the rat's in the hat!" The crowd was delirious. This is what they had come to see.

"Is that why you cheated on Fabio?" Matt asked Maria.

"Yes, I thought I might get AIDS."

"But you didn't know he had a gay boyfriend." Matt pointed out the obvious inconsistency – to the huge and raucous delight of the audience. The chant went up again.

The show ended with Matt reading some pious platitudes from autocue; this was designed to give the show a veneer of moral legitimacy it so clearly lacked. He rattled off the clichés in an insincere monotone that indicated he was casting pearls before swine – if indeed they were pearls.

On the afternoon of the following Friday the blue-visaged man from New Jersey came to see Matt in his office on the pretext of potential sponsorship. He sat opposite Matt and very soon dropped the front.

"I didn't like the show on Wednesday," he said.

"May I ask why?" Matt inquired, his pulse rate rising a little. This wasn't the meeting he expected.

"Maria is my daughter."

"Who?"

"You don't even know, do you?"

"Oh, the pregnant girl... Yes, I see..." He took a sip of water and offered to pour a glass for the angry man sitting opposite him.

"They're not real people to you, are they? Maria, my daughter, now wants to terminate her pregnancy. Have you any idea of the harm you do with that dumb show?"

"It was her decision to come on the show. She signed a release. And the terms and conditions are..."

"These legal niceties don't bother me... I work in refuse disposal..."

"I don't see the relevance..." Matt, however, wasn't being completely honest. He had gone on tilt and he struggled to conceal any signs of unease.

"We make things disappear. Deep in landfill."

Matt's heart began to pound. "I'll ... I'll have to call security."

"Go ahead. But let me tell you what I want. I want you to end the show. Now. Take it off the air."

"You can't come in here and make demands..." This man worried about sensitivities but had no qualms about having people clipped. Not family of course. But that made it worse.

"I'll leave you my card." The heavy-set man stood and left.

That evening Matt relayed the experience to Barb. They both studied the business card, which showed the man as CEO of one of the foremost refuse companies in the city. Two acronyms were scribbled in ink on top of the card.

Barb read out the first one, "I k w y l." She read it a number of times, then took in a sharp breath and went pale. She pushed the remains of her evening meal away from her.

"What's the matter?" Matt inquired. "What is it?"

"Don't you get it? 'I know where you live'." She went to peer through a chink in the curtain of the dining-room window at the street outside. Of all the risks she had worried about – legal writs, Matt's growing lethargy, sinking or collapsing ratings – this one had never entered her mind.

Matt was concerned, but it all seemed too melodramatic in a way, almost like a vendetta. He puzzled over the second acronym, 'I o h t b l o'. Barb tried to decipher it too, but was unsuccessful, mainly because she was too upset to think straight.

It was just after they'd kissed and were trying to go asleep that the answer came to her. She sat bolt upright in bed.

"Christ!"

"What?" He sat up as well.

"I only have to be lucky once."

In petrified silence they both stared into the dark of their well-furnished bedroom.

MANY AND OFTEN

I WAS TALKING TO MY WIFE, Gemma, in a speakeasy and we were both laughing, she more than me. My humour was a little restrained for a very good reason. My wife, Gemma, died four years ago, having been swept over a cliff in a catastrophic mud slide.

Yet here she was, not a double or doppelgänger, but the real Gemma exactly as I remembered her. And here was I, large as life. All of my senses were focused on details of her appearance, voice, intonation – and everything checked out. This was Gemma. There was no question about it. Other things around us seemed different; some of the cocktails looked very strange and exotic, the décor was unusual, and the barman who served us seemed more like a professor. But Gemma was Gemma. And it was not a dream.

Maybe it was some kind of magical moment but I wanted it to last. I was afraid she might disappear if I acted strangely. So I tried to act normal.

She was talking about the time our young son got a crayon stuck in his nose and we used pepper to get him to sneeze it down.

"What colour was the crayon?" I asked.

"Green. Don't you remember? It's not that long ago."

"But the pepper didn't work…"

"No. We had to bring him to the ER. And when he saw this large Matron coming towards him with tubes and a big rubber bulb, he cried so much, the crayon came flying out."

"It was so funny," I said. "And what did he call the matron on the way home in the car?"

"'Bad Lady, bad lady,' he kept saying."

I looked at the fingernail of her left thumb. She's always had difficulty keeping the cuticle from encroaching on the half moon. It checked out. Her ring finger was exactly the same length as the index finger. I also noticed the cow's lick, that piece of stray hair at the front which she always found difficult to control. The laughter that lurked near the surface of her pale blue eyes was still there.

"Remind me how you got that little scar there." I pointed to the back of her right hand.

She looked curiously at me. "Is your memory playing tricks. I told you before it was from a pellet gun."

"Oh, that little guy you used to play with, Johnny, Johnny somebody."

"Tommy Kernan," she corrected me. "How much have you had to drink, Larry?"

Jesus, what was going on? I remembered stooping over the coffin to kiss her goodbye. There wasn't a day in the last four years that I didn't think about her – and think about ending my own life. Oh yes, I had a Glock and a bottle of whiskey at the ready in the bedroom.

"You must remember Tommy," she went on.

"He was the wildest of the bunch. He used to throw lit matches into mail boxes just for the fun of it."

My head was lifting. Should I ask her to bed – the ultimate test. No, not fair and no need. I had proof enough – every minute detail checked out. But proof of what? That she hadn't really died? No, I had watched as the coffin was lowered into the grave. Resurrection was a myth. Gods only. Maybe I'd died and this was the hoped-for meeting in Heaven? I looked around the sleazy bar. If this was Heaven why was I so worried and confused?

I had to make my fears explicit.

"You might think I'm mad," I said, "but were you ever caught in a mud slide?"

She looked and laughed. "Is that what it was? I just remember being caught up in some powerful force. Larry, what's this about? I feel you're testing me or something."

It took a while to summon my courage. "Four years ago you died in a mud slide. Your car was swept over a cliff. There was a funeral…" I couldn't go on. Instead I studied her reaction, hoping she wouldn't be too offended or shocked.

"I thought it was something like that." She didn't seem fazed at all.

"But you're here … in this bar … having a drink with me."

"I certainly am. Isn't it extraordinary?" She clicked her glass against mine.

"But how … I mean…?"

I waited for an explanation but suddenly everything changed. I was in bed in my apartment on Bleecker Street, listening to traffic sluicing the wet streets. I hadn't just woken up; therefore I hadn't been dreaming. I searched high and low but there was no sign of Gemma. The suddenness of our parting meant that I had no coordinates for her. What in hell was going on? I felt as if some displacement had taken place, a slippage in the order of things. I poured myself a stiff drink and fed the cat. I switched on the TV and watched a rerun of a sitcom I'd seen a couple of years ago. The implied continuity gave me reassurance. But I wondered if I would ever meet Gemma again or whether she had slipped back to her normal condition of nonexistence. Days and weeks of misery piled up ahead of me.

I did meet her again, a few weeks later, by sheer luck. On the subway.

"Do you know the odds against meeting again like this?" she asked in a disbelieving tone of voice.

"Well, New York is a big place," I began. I was delighted to see her again and asked her to join me in a mid-morning cup of coffee. The subway station was on top of the building that housed the coffee shop. We were served by a barista who looked very like the professorial barman in the speakeasy.

She was laughing quietly to herself. I had always liked her enigmatic and idiosyncratic sense of humour. "What's so funny?"

"This isn't New York. But I know what you mean. Your estimate of the odds against meeting is far too low."

"I don't follow." My eyes roved over her face; I needed more clues.

"Imagine a large forest. There's a massive explosion which uproots and severs all the trees. After the explosion what do they find? The exploded forest has formed a city of beautiful log-houses, each with its own front garden and yard."

"That couldn't happen," I said.

"It could," she insisted. "Meeting you today is as unlikely as that."

I weighed this up quickly and with a heavy heart. "If that's true and we part company today, we'll probably never meet again? Is that what you're saying?"

"I'm afraid so."

I became very nervous. If the slippage happened again I would lose her forever. My concern produced burning physical pain.

"Is there anything we can do to prevent parting again? There must be something."

She shook her head sadly. "No, nothing. That's just how it is."

"Gemma, what's going on? I don't want to

lose you... You were always the smart one... You must have a theory..."

"Well, Larry, all I know is that the scientists were partly right. There isn't just one universe. There's an infinity of them. There's an infinity of every one of us.

I had a sudden recollection of my old math teacher who used to say, "Zero is a troublesome brute but infinity takes the cake." He used to talk about Hilbert's Hotel which had an infinite number of rooms. Even when it was full it could accommodate extra guests. Or could it? There was a question I had to ask.

"Are you Gemma or not?"

"Yes and no. Your wife is dead. But I am the same woman in a different universe. You have somehow entered this universe which is highly unusual, virtually impossible."

"All I know is that I love you."

"That's because I'm the same woman as Gemma. So I love you too."

"But how can people go from one universe to another?"

The barista stopped at our table and joined the conversation, much to my annoyance. "The universe we're most used to," he said, "is like a radio station that we have tuned into. There is an infinity of other stations but we don't know how to tune into them. But, my suspicion is that for some unknown reason, we can accidentally move into another universe. I think that's what happened to you. I have the image of paint on a canvas bleeding into a different colour. But it can bleed out as well."

"And can we delay bleeding out?" I asked the barista, even though I half wished he'd go away and leave us alone.

"No, I don't think so." He shook his head slowly.

"So there's an infinity of Gemmas out there and an infinity of me?"

"Minus one – because the Gemma from your planet is dead. But I think that's still infinity."

"And are we all exactly the same?"

"Yes, in the essentials such as DNA and body type. It's very unusual to have visitors from other planets," he said. "The branes must have touched in some way."

"Branes?" I queried.

"Membranes," Gemma explained. "This is Marco by the way."

"Yes," Marco explained. "It's the latest term for the multiverse. Long gone are the days when we thought our galaxy, Alpha Centauri, *was* the entire universe."

"We used to think that the Milky Way was all there was." I looked from one to the other. Was there something between them? "Are you...? Do you know one another?"

They both laughed and Gemma explained, "On this planet we don't wait to be introduced. Everyone talks to everyone else."

"That's wonderful," I said, continuing to hope that the chatty barista would go away and let me talk to Gemma on my own. I was all too conscious of how short our time together might be. I caught a glimpse of my reflection in a sort of glitter ball behind the bar and lost count of how many self-images I detected.

"Yes, this is called the sociable planet..."

The next thing I heard was my cat meowing on a countertop of my kitchen. I gave her a saucer of milk knowing sadly that I had bled out.

I sat in an easy chair and let darkness fill the flat.

Over the next few days I went through another grieving process for Gemma, but then I had the consolation of knowing that at least she survived on other planets in other universes. I stroked the cat and was filled with a feeling of deep contentment that matched her purrs. There was much to be said for the multiverse and for infinity. I began to see that uniqueness was overrated.

NOT JUST THE COLOUR

"I DON'T UNDERSTAND," Paul Molloy said as he looked at the salesman's card. "It says 'Eamonn Ó Dubhail' here."

"That's right," the salesman laughed. Eddie Doyle. Sometimes I use the Irish version. It doesn't hurt to do your bit for the old Erse, you know."

"I suppose not." Paul slipped the card into his wallet.

They had just completed two test drives. He had put the new car through its paces and found it smooth and spirited. Eddie Doyle had tested the car to be traded in and found it to be showing its age, 'just like himself'. They spent some time after that in the brightly lit showroom, going over the figures, until Eddie said that a particular figure was the best he could do. To do more would take the flesh off his back. Paul agreed; the figure was not unreasonable. It would cost him €9,750 to change. Eddie wrote the figure down on the card that Paul had just put in his wallet.

"It's a pity you don't have the Sahara Gold version in stock," Paul said.

"It'll only take two weeks to order one. It's a very popular colour with the ladies this year, especially the metallic paint." Eddie pointed to a fire-engine red version near the front window of the showroom; it was tied in a huge pink silk bow. "You could drive that baby out of here right now. This instant."

Paul looked and cogitated. His wife really preferred Sahara Gold and she was inclined to think all shades of red were too loud.

Eddie offered him his mobile phone. "Do you want to discuss it with the little woman?"

"No." Paul made a decision. "We'll wait for the Sahara Gold. Two weeks?"

"Two weeks." Eddie stood and held out his hand; they shook on the deal.

A month later there was no sign of the car. Whenever Paul rang to inquire whether it had arrived, Eddie would reply, "It's still on the high seas."

"But you said it would be here in two weeks."

"I know, but these things happen. We had the order in in good time. Maybe they mislaid it. Anyway they missed the shipment. But it's on the high seas as we speak."

More weeks went by and the car was still on the high seas. Paul's wife opined one evening that the car must have gone on a voyage more circuitous by far than that of Ulysses. Paul had a mental image of the Sahara Gold vehicle lashed to the deck of a ship in the teeth of a storm, rounding the Cape of Good Hope.

Sometime later Eddie rang Paul at the office.

"I have good news and bad news," he said. "The good news is I have the car."

"That's great." Paul visualised the brave little

car at last on terra firma. "What's the bad news?"

"The price has gone up by €700."

"What?"

"Yeah, it's too bad. There was a price increase in the offing. We just got caught."

Paul swallowed hard. "*We* got caught. *I* got caught you mean." He wasn't thinking straight and needed more time. There was something wrong. In fact the more he thought about it the more it stank. "Wait now, we had a deal, €9,750 to change…"

"That's now €10,450 when you add on the €700."

The fact that the salesman was doing the arithmetic for him was the last straw – did he think he was dealing with a moron? Paul was slow to anger and never liked to give vent to it, so now he had the problem of controlling the adrenalin that surged through him.

"We had a deal … we shook on it."

"There was nothing in writing." Eddie countered. His voice had suddenly lost its joshing, pally quality.

"The number is written down on your card." With his free hand Paul shook the card from his wallet on to the desk. "I'm looking at it. €9,750 is the figure … in *your* handwriting." He was conscious of a slight tremor in his voice, which could be construed as a sign of weakness, and he fought to control it.

"That's neither here nor there. We only had a handshake agreement…"

"Only ... *only* ... a handshake..." Paul began to babble. "It's still ... binding ... under the law."

"But you'd have to *prove* it." Eddie said. "Look, if you don't want to pay the price I won't hold you to the deal. I'll sell the car to someone else."

"I have to ... talk to my solicitor. Don't sell that car ... to anyone else... I'm hanging up now." Paul threw his cell phone on the desk and tried to calm himself.

A colleague dropped into the office and Paul told him the story with as much control as he could muster.

"It's rough out there," the colleague said in a lilting tone. He seemed to be suggesting that Paul was some kind of neophyte who didn't understand the cut and thrust of the market place. He made matters worse by adding, "You need to wear tight underwear to keep alert out there."

Over the coming days Paul spoke to his solicitor over the phone. He outlined his slowly-forming opinion that they had deliberately delayed the sale of the car *until* the price increase had come through. They had probably stalled on many other deals as well for the same reason. The more he thought about it the more convinced Paul became that it wasn't bad luck or a coincidence, it was a carefully worked out scam. The car had not been on the high seas at all; it had been hidden in a warehouse with all the other models waiting for the price to rise.

The solicitor advised caution in making such allegations; they could rebound on him.

"It's a murky area," he said.

Paul unburdened himself to his wife about the car, his unsympathetic colleague, the ineffectual lawyer.

"You should have taken the red car," she said.

"I what...? You hate red."

"Yes, but in the circumstances..." She made a moue. Again, there was that faint implication that he really didn't know how to comport himself in the real world; that he was fair game.

"The circumstances only became clear *afterwards*..."

"There's no need to raise your voice, Dear. I'm just trying to help." She looked at him as if she had difficulty recognising who he was.

Paul went to bed early, tossed, turned and cursed under his breath.

He rang Eddie the next morning and threatened him with a solicitor's letter.

"Fire away," Eddie said. "They make no difference. We're well used to filing them away in the waste bin. I think I have a buyer for the car."

"Don't sell it." Paul warned him. "It's mine."

"At the new price."

"At the old price ... the price we agreed on."

"Sorry. No can do." A click was followed by a dial tone.

"Don't hang up on me, you bastard," Paul

said to no one in particular. He opened a drawer, pulled out a sheet of paper and began to set out a plan of campaign. Like most backroom boys he was much better on paper than on his feet. Maybe people were right; the marketplace was not his natural habitat.

After fifteen minutes the pages were swarming with ideas, generated by a desire for justice, vengeance, face-saving and filthy lucre. His motives were hopelessly mixed and some were downright unworthy. The latter bothered him slightly; he hadn't fully realised how nasty he could be, but he came to regard it as a strength. After another half hour a strategy emerged. He was not just good on paper but damned good, and he vowed to stick to that medium.

The first letter was to the Chief Executive of the Motor Distributors. It was a model of subtle accusation, sarcasm and veiled threat. Paul felt much better after writing it and he almost enjoyed the process of buying the stamp and sending it off in the mail. Letter-writing had the great advantage of avoiding human contact. Also it was clear-cut. You stated your case, chose the appropriate tone and allowed for possible reactions. Indeed, as a skilful letter-writer Paul felt he could set little traps for his correspondent to fall into. He was a puppet-master, manipulating his creatures from a safe distance. Emails just didn't allow for the same subtlety or formality.

As it turned out the Chief Executive did rise to the bait in his reply which dropped through Paul's letterbox four days later. It was a robust defence of "company policy" which asserted that any suggestion of "sharp practice" could only be regarded as "reprehensible." The word 'reprehensible' hit Paul between the eyes. He almost staggered backwards from the thrust. And he knew it was going to get rougher before it got better. He kept returning to the letter as if he were picking at a sore. On waking in the middle of the night he sneaked downstairs to see if that word was still in the letter. It was, and the Chief Executive had the temerity to invite Paul to seek legal redress, if he felt so inclined, knowing of course that the law was worse than useless and that solicitors and barristers were lazy fee-mongers.

His wife woke when he got back into bed. "Why don't you let it go? Tell them to shove the car. Go to another garage and buy a different one."

"It's my car," he said stubbornly. "Sahara Gold." He wasn't sure why he added that. "I hate them for trying this on me. But, if they want to do it the hard way, that's all right by me."

"I'd forget about it," his wife said.

"Not me. I'll show them who they're up against." Later that night he dreamed of setting fire to a showroom full of shiny new cars; a few salesmen went up like roman candles in the conflagration and ended up as charred greasy blobs on the floor. When he woke in the morning he wasn't sure if it had been a dream or some kind of augury. No, he wouldn't go that far, or would be? He was finding things out about himself that were strange and not exactly praiseworthy.

He was on some kind of high as he composed many different replies to the Chief Executive. The combination of writing and adrenalin put him in the zone. God, he was good. He chose the best draft and polished it. The main point of the letter was that he would not bother with legal action but would instead go to the media. Let the court of public opinion decide. He also added a few little barbs including a reference to the salesman, Mr. Eddie Doyle *aka Eamonn Ó Dubhail*. He particularly liked that touch and felt sure that the inference was clear enough, viz. that people who slipped from one name into another, pretending they were doing it "for the sake of the old Erse" had something to hide.

The response which duly arrived was a little calmer in tone than its predecessor (or maybe Paul was growing a thicker skin) but it more or less accused him of bluffing. He went in for the kill.

His next letter was a complete work of fiction but all the better for that. He told the Chief Executive that he was on very good terms with the producer of a well-known consumer affairs programme on TV. This producer (who had in fact an excellent reputation for muckraking) was only too keen to "investigate" the motor trade. In addition, he, Paul, would write to the Motor (and other) Correspondents of the print media. He would publish a letter in *The Times* setting out what had happened to him and inviting other readers who had been similarly treated to contact him. He would also go on the Joe Duffy phone-in radio programme. Finally, he was copying the letter to the President of the Motor Company in Tokyo.

He sent the letter off and waited. This was his best effort. He knew it would be impossible to top it. If he were the recipient of a letter like that he would need several changes of underwear before he got through the first paragraph. He didn't have to wait long for a response but it didn't come through the mail.

Eddie rang him one morning. He sounded breezy, "Hi, Paul, about that car business, why don't you drop in so we can talk?"

"There's nothing to talk about."

"We could compromise. Split the difference maybe."

"No. We had a deal. Either it stands or it doesn't." On a sudden impulse he added, "*An dtuigeann tú é sin?*"

"What?"

"*An dtuigeann tú é sin?*"

"I don't know what you're saying."

"Goodbye, Mr. Ó Duibhil." Paul rang off. He had two reasons to gloat.

That evening over dinner his wife picked up

on his changed mood. He admitted that "the car thing" was beginning to work itself out.

"I had to come the heavy," he said, forking up some vegetables. "There was no alternative. Bullies and conmen of that sort have to be taken on and confronted. You have to show them who's boss."

She gave him a strange look.

It was of course inevitable that Eddie would ring again. There were no pleasantries this time. He simply said, "You can have the car."

On Saturday morning over breakfast Paul asked his wife if she would go in and collect the new car. He said he was afraid of what he might say or do to the infamous twice-named salesman.

"You mean you'd find it awkward?"

"Well ... maybe."

"Face-to-face contact?" she pressed.

"It wouldn't be ... easy." He conceded.

She got her coat and bag and as she was leaving to pick up the Sahara Gold car, she gave him a peck on the cheek.

"Welcome back," she said.

PANOPTIC FLY

THE STAFF HAD DUSTED and polished the room earlier that day, and were now putting out the stacking chairs in rows facing the podium. The room was being prepared for the AGM of St. Martin's Golf Club.

I settled myself by the window to watch the members arrive. All the drivers were very careful not to park in the Captain's or President's spot. It was a bright autumn evening and the artisans used the opportunity of the AGM to play a few holes. One of the young lads, Cummiskey, was a greatly talented golfer; I watched him auger his drive about 300 yards straight down the third fairway on a rising curve, fading it at the end into the dog leg which opened up the green for his approach shot. It was a par 5 and he would definitely make a birdie, if not an eagle. I know about flight paths and performance in air. Cummiskey was a master in the making.

A few members were already in the bar, getting in a few drinks before the meeting. I picked up some of the conversation. One was advising the others to buy shares in a certain company; he had it on good authority that the company was about to be taken over.

In another group a large man known as the Judge, though he was only a Senior Counsel, was posing over the Agenda for the AGM, advising his listeners that the Secretary hadn't safe hands, was a bit of a troublemaker, and might try to sell the pass on one or two of the Agenda items.

I saw the Captain park in his reserved spot. He got out of the car and stood for a while looking out at the course. I thought at first he was admiring the view, which was quite beautiful in the slanting bronze sunlight. Then, going by the motions of his finger, I could see that he was counting the number of players who were on the course. When he'd finished the count he looked at his watch and wrote something in a small notebook. On closer inspection I was able to decipher "At 5.25 p.m. Tuesday, 27 September, 2010 I counted 12 artisans out, some on the 6th hole. Must have started at 4.30 p.m., a full hour before permitted time. Take up with President." I knew, however, that he was uncertain as to whether the President would take it quite as seriously as he did. He sighed, put the notebook back into his pocket and entered the club house, through the locker room which he liked to inspect from time to time.

He took his Captaincy seriously and even more seriously once his name went on the honour plaque in gold leaf. It would be there for all time over the mantelpiece of the Members' Bar. St. Martin's Golf Club had become his life; not suddenly, but gradually as his other interests fell away. And occasionally he wondered if there might be any way, without appearing superficial, of renaming it, *Royal* St. Martin's. *Royal and Ancient* would be too much, but *Royal* would hit the spot. He knew that a majority of members shared his view but they were, to one degree or another, a little coy about approaching the Golf Union of Ireland with such a proposal.

The meeting room was almost full by 6 p.m. and the President used his gavel to bring the meeting to order. The Agenda was agreed and the Minutes of the last meeting were approved with one or two finicky amendments which the Secretary took on board with a poor grace. One of these related to disallowing Tax Inspectors from becoming members. The Captain said that while he agreed with the proposal, it was written too explicitly and it should be fudged a bit. "Tax Inspectors" was finally deleted and the sentence changed to give the Membership Committee all due power to decide on the suitability of applicants and their compatibility with the core values of the Club.

The President looked at his watch. They were making reasonable progress. With any luck he'd be out of there by 8 p.m. and be able to keep the appointment for a light supper with his mistress in her flat at 9-ish. He had two bottles of claret in the boot of his Mercedes. He sometimes wondered why he accepted the Presidency; he wasn't even that fond of golf, though he needed the exercise. Still, when they all asked him to take on the honorary position and praised him for his business acumen he found it difficult to refuse.

"Now we have the Report of the

Handicapping Committee." The President held it aloft and riffled through the pages. "I must say it makes sense to me." He pretended he'd read it but looked to the Captain for confirmation.

"I have no difficulties with it, Mr. President." That was his usual conciliatory introduction which he then proceeded to qualify. "I do, however, wonder if James Howlett has been cut enough. I would have thought 16 a bit generous. Perhaps 14 would be more appropriate."

The Secretary objected on the grounds that the handicaps were worked out scrupulously on the basis of competition scores.

"So what do you base your view on?" the President asked.

"Observation," the Captain said. "I've seen him do Amen Corner in level par several times."

Judging by the groans and murmurs the committee members were divided on the issue. The Secretary's method was more scientific and up to date but observation had served them well over the years. A lively debate from the floor ensued. The Judge expressed a strong preference for the more traditional method.

The President sneaked a look at this watch. They really should put a clock on the far wall to avoid the need for such indiscreet gestures. The image of Sheila letting her dress drop from her shoulders and then stepping out of the satiny puddle on the floor played itself over and over in his mind. He brought the gavel down. "I propose fifteen. Show of hands please."

It was unusual to ask for a vote at such an early stage in the debate and some of the hands were slow to go up. Finally the Secretary did a count.

"Motion carried. James Howlett's handicap has been fixed at 15."

"Let it be so noted in the minutes." The Captain, none too pleased, insisted on having the last word. The Secretary made a token mark with a biro in the margin of the minute book. I came closer to take a look and was waved away by a liver-spotted hand.

"Now we turn to the item on membership," the president announced, "and as you all know the hoary issue of gender raises its head once again."

"I sometimes despair of the times we're living in," the Captain said with a deep sigh. When the murmur of approbation from the body of the hall had died down, the Secretary cleared his throat and began to talk about the necessity of keeping up with the times. Then he adopted a more practical argument. "Remember, unless we remove the ban on female members we won't have any access to Lottery funds."

"We can raise our own funds," the Judge called out. He went on to explain how frustrating it was to find oneself playing behind a female four-ball. Apart from all the duffed shots, they spent most of the time nattering and admiring the views. They ruined the game for men. It wasn't their fault of course; they behaved as the Good

Lord made them. That was why they were so lovable. Murmurs of approval swelled to a cheer by the time he'd finished.

"We've always been self-sufficient. And remember, we have huge equity in the club. The land is priceless." This second voice was also greeted positively.

"Anyway it's a private club," another member said. "We don't have to feel guilty about our policy. Imagine if one of us tried to join the Irish Countrywomen's Association? We'd soon be shown the door."

More voices were cut off by the President, who asked for a show of hands.

"But we haven't really debated the issue," the Captain said with a stronger tone of reprimand than he intended.

There was no need for a count; almost every paw was raised. Women were denied full membership for another year at least.

Pavilion membership was then discussed. There was one vacancy since the untimely death of Father Monaghan. The Captain mentioned the name of a close friend and, despite the fact that he was 65th on the waiting list, he was leapfrogged to the front. No vote was needed. The Captain and President had certain unquestioned rights. Even so, the Captain rationalised his choice of new Pavilion member on the grounds that he was a good friend of the Minister for Sport.

"Enough said," the Secretary exclaimed with

barely concealed sarcasm that attracted the attention of many present. Even the President turned sideways to read his expression.

Some members at the back of the hall were having drinks served surreptitiously to them. There wasn't much noise but the President had a horror of the meeting being prolonged if drink was made available.

"Gentlemen, could I ask you to wait until the meeting is over before ordering drinks?" He softened the rebuke by reminding them that since they had a private club liquor license they could stay in the bar for as long as they liked afterwards. He, himself, would of course be in a far better place. In fact he had to force himself to concentrate on the Agenda to prevent a painful bulge developing in his tweed trousers.

"We're still on the question of membership," he reminded them. Suddenly an image of his wife's frank face swam before his eyes and he felt the full force of how he was betraying her and the kids. But he couldn't help it, human nature being what it was.

One of the Judge's cronies reported a very unseemly event that occurred on the previous Saturday. A relatively new member had been seen taking a practice swing *after* hitting his ball and he hadn't replaced *either* divot.

"I think I know who you mean," the Captain said, "and I saw the same … person… ignore his own pitch mark on the 14th green. This isn't just a matter of protocol or etiquette. It's a clear violation of the rules. I don't think we have any option but to expel him."

"Who are we talking about?" the Secretary inquired frowning. Even in a kangaroo court the defendant should be named.

"We'll tell you that later," the Captain said. "The matter will be dealt with discreetly."

The Secretary protested and argued for a compromise; a reprimand, instead of expulsion. He had little support.

"A slap on the wrist?" the Judge queried "For two divots and at least one pitch mark? No, Sir. Not a chance."

So the still unnamed member was expelled and another name was suggested. The Secretary intervened, his face burning from earlier encounters.

"I think we should make young Cummiskey a member. He plays off two and will soon be a scratch player. We have to encourage talent like that."

There was a long silence. Eventually the Captain spoke very judiciously. "Believe me, I have nothing against young Cummiskey or indeed any of the artisans, but we have to be careful. Careful about tradition and careful about creating precedents that could have implications which we cannot foresee at the present moment…" He left his words hanging in the air; it was someone else's turn to take over the torch.

"But surely," the Secretary persisted, "we have a responsibility to nurture talent. With proper training Cummiskey could be a Ryder cup player."

"I must say, I'm inclined to agree with the Captain," the Judge said in a most philosophical tone, as if he had spent years agonising over this particular moral dilemma.

"On balance I agree with the Judge," another voice piped up. "Golf is more than a game; it's a ... form of cultural activity."

The President asked for a vote. The young Cummiskey was deemed unsuitable for membership, though he could of course continue to play during those hours reserved for artisans and caddies.

"I assume there's no other business," the President said. "I declare the meeting over. Thank you all very much."

An informal buzz of chatter broke out and the suspended drinks' orders were reactivated. The President found it more difficult than he thought to make good his departure. There was back-slapping and congratulations on his efficient chairmanship. He was offered drinks and declined. "I'll get you again. Have to be off now."

Finally he escaped. As he sat into his powerful car he mused on the full-bodied success of his life.

The Secretary packed his briefcase, sat for a while nursing a lager, then he too left. He was seen leaving by the Judge and his group. No words were spoken for a while; facial expressions were enough to indicate that they wanted a more clubbable Secretary. When they began to speak I hovered as close as I could. With his rolled-up agenda the Judge caught me off guard with a sudden and painful swat. I kept my distance after that.

SPORTSWOMANSHIP

THE COMMENTATOR NEARLY JUMPED out of his box when, in the opening minutes of the Six Nations' Women's Final, he saw Ireland's Number Five, Stella Rattigan, soar like an eagle, steal the ball in the line-out and then, with help from the Number Eight, Rita O'Hagan, and others, push the English women over the line. It was the most extraordinary try he had seen in his lifetime. The Irish maul was a Panzer tank, pushing everything out of its way. The English players tried to collapse it but failed.

The Irish defence pushed forward relentlessly. The ball-carriers, especially Stella and Rita, ploughed into the English defenders and crossed the gain line time after time. He saw Stella cross the whitewash with an English defender hanging on to each of her legs. The English Captain complained to the Referee that in the build-up there had been a forward pass but she didn't entertain it.

By half time the commentator was hoarse from shouting. The score was 21-0 in favour of Ireland, who were now almost certain to win the Grand Slam. At the start of the second half England had replaced the Hooker and the Full-back. But it made little difference. The unchanged Irish side hammered into them, winning almost all of the set pieces, regardless of who had the put-in.

Early in the half Rita O'Hagan cleaned out yet another ruck and passed the ball to her Winger, who scored a walk-in try. "This is absolutely brilliant stuff!" the commentator yelled into the mic; more precise analysis would have to wait for later.

Whether rucking, tackling, or packing down, the Irish were completely on top, largely because of Stella and Rita, who helped create tries from the base of the scrum or crossed the line themselves. The heads of the English players began to drop.

On one occasion Rita received a pass near midfield and instead of charging through or passing it out, she attempted a drop kick, almost as a joke. As the ball soared between the posts she grinned to show it was just a try-on, albeit one that succeeded. After the restart, England won the ball and one of their well-built Flankers began to barge through. She was tackled by Stella, upended, and forced to spill the ball.

Some overzealous rucking resulted in an English player being stretchered off. A penalty was awarded to England and their Fly-half succeeded in kicking it over.

The game ended with a scoreline of 55–3. The Aviva Stadium was in an uproar, the commentator lost his voice and croaked his way during the award ceremony. The Irish Women's team had more than compensated for the poor showing of their male counterparts that season. From now on the women's game would, according to the commentator, attract as much attention as the men's game, if not more. We were, he continued, witnessing history in the making. The Guinness award for best player went to Stella Rattigan, who graciously accepted the lanyard around her neck and the glass trophy.

The mood in the English changing room was miserable. The team had been put through the wringer, and their bruises were painful. A winning side didn't feel bruises.

"Well, you tried your best," The coach tried to console them. "But the Irish girls were better on the day. It happens." He had no intention of berating them for errors.

These postmatch platitudes elicited no response from the dejected players, so he tried again, "I never saw anything like the performance of their Numbers Five and Eight. It was unprecedented."

Again, no response. The captain sat with head in hands, remembering how she had been virtually lifted out of a ruck and flung away by Stella Rattigan. She'd never experienced anything quite like it. It was as if her seventy-kilo fit body was just a piece of fluff. She had seen her Scrum-half being tackled so hard that her mouthguard flew out of her mouth. And it was a fair tackle. But, Jesus, the force of it! She could hardly blame her defenders for drifting and sliding off half-hearted tackles. They had been beaten up as well as beaten. And the coach, who no doubt meant well, was simply unable to cheer anyone up.

In the Irish changing room there was jubilation and frequent discharges of shaken-up bubbly. Winning the Grand Slam by beating the old enemy was heady stuff indeed, especially with an incredible margin of 52 points. Adrenaline still coursed freely in veins. The coach lavished praise on them all; he didn't want to single out Stella and Rita, but everyone was fully aware of the mega shifts they had put in.

"No crowing over them at dinner tonight," the coach warned.

"As if we would," Stella said to waves of laughter.

"Ah, I know you wouldn't," the coach replied. "You're all good sports."

On the bus back to the hotel the captain of the English side chatted with the coach and at last voiced her true opinion, based on the sheer power of Ireland's two star players.

"I know what you're getting at," the coach told her. "But you've no proof."

"It wasn't just the way they played," she said into his ear. "When we shook hands after the game, I couldn't believe how big their hands were … and there's something else too…"

"I don't want to hear it." The coach turned aside and watched the colour-bedecked crowds thronging the streets in search of hostelries for celebration and commiseration.

"You have to…"

"Look, let's just enjoy dinner tonight. Put it

behind us, as they say, and move on."

"But we're talking about fairness here…"

"Look, if you raise this issue we'll be accused of being poor losers. It's not on."

The captain grabbed him by the arm and whispered, "You should know this … In a few of the scrums I copped a feel…"

"You did what? I can't believe what you're saying."

"You know very well what I'm saying. Family jewels were all present and accounted for."

He looked around him to make sure they were not being overheard by the other players. "I don't care. It makes no difference. I mentioned our sporting reputation already. Do you want us to be accused of transphobia as well?"

"The hell with political correctness, Coach. We were fucked over by those players. We have to make a formal complaint."

"Not on my watch." He screened her out with his headphones and piped music selection.

In the Irish changing room Stella and Rita waited until their teammates had finished, before going for their showers.

"I really enjoyed that game," Stella said, working up an inch-deep lather of spray-on soap.

"Me too." Rita relived the joy of running through other players without any knockbacks. And of course there was the huge continuing bonus of living one's life as a woman, which was her compelling goal since she was ten years old.

"Is that a new shampoo?" Stella inquired.

"Yes, *Moonlight Gleam.* Would you like to try it? I prefer it to *Jojoba.*"

Stella applied it liberally to her hair and said that she loved the feel and scent, which was lemony and springlike. Then she asked a little out of the blue, "Do you think what we're doing is fair?"

"Oh, not that again, Stella. Of course it's fair. We're women, aren't we? And we deliberately held back in the earlier games this season. Look, gender is a state of mind. We all know that now."

"I suppose you're right." Stella handed back the shampoo. "I suppose I just need to be reassured every now and again. I'm only six foot four and wouldn't be tall enough for the line-out in the men's game."

"Well, consider yourself lucky that you're now a woman... By the way, I was invited to be interviewed on TV. It'll be broadcast next week."

"What are you going to say?"

"The truth. There's nothing to be defensive about, not in today's liberal climate. I mean, we're transgenders not criminals, for God's sake." She moisturised her legs vigorously.

Stella emerged from the hot shower. "Right on, Rita. And good luck."

Dinner that evening was a low-key affair, but after a certain level of wine consumption, singing commenced. Stella's rendition of 'Carrickfergus' in a baritone register did not go down very well with the English team, the members of which did not go to the Ladies when Stella or Rita happened to be using the facilities. Later in the evening some veiled aspersions were cast – and the English captain pointedly asked Stella what kind of gym training she used to develop her quads and glutes – but the coaches prevented the matter from escalating. As the event broke up in the early hours of the morning, the English coach made a short speech in which he promised to give Ireland a better game next year.

Early the following week, Rita did her interview with RTÉ, and quickly cut to the chase, saying that she was a 'Trans' player. The interviewer asked if she thought that conferred an unfair advantage. Rita replied that everyone had an advantage in something or other. Some athletes were very tall and had an advantage in the high jump, an endowment of quick-twitch muscles made others very good at sprinting. A writer might be blessed by a vivid imagination, and so on.

"Yes…" the interviewer pressed, "but those advantages are…" He hesitated and added, "natural…"

"Are you suggesting that gender preference and sexual identity are not natural?" Rita promptly inquired. "I might point out that at present, seventy-eight different genders are recognised."

The Producer spoke into the interviewer's earpiece. "Be very careful, Liam ... dangerous territory ... withdraw the word 'natural'. Do it now!"

The interviewer said he had "misspoken"; he asked a few more innocuous questions and the interview ended in smiles. The interviewer again congratulated Rita on her spectacular performance against the English team.

After a summer of highly volatile weather in that corner of Europe where six nations love the oval ball, training began again. The English team had the same coach, who somehow managed to ride out the bad press he received over the humiliating defeat in the Aviva Stadium. He had brought in several new players, much to the annoyance of the captain, who buttonholed him one morning on the touch line just before a squad training session.

"It's very disruptive to bring in so much new blood in one fell swoop," she said. "And it's demoralising to lose so many of our close colleagues."

"You think...?" He was growing a little tired of her constant criticisms, which all missed the big picture as far as he was concerned.

"Yes." She was still mad at him for not lodging a formal complaint after the Irish game, and she began to think of him as a weakling, a bureaucrat afraid to rock the boat.

"The game is changing," he said.

"I know ... stronger defences, pod formations..."

"The world is changing." He spread his hands, and stared into the middle distance, to indicate that he was dealing with larger issues.

"Meaning?"

"We have to fight fire with fire. You may not have noticed yet that most of the new players are transgender women."

"Christ, you can't do that."

He said that it was a done deal and that her position on the team was by no means certain. It wasn't clear how a cis-gender woman could motivate a transgender team. He told her that in time there might be a separate 'Transgender' competition and a separate 'Cis-women's' one. There might even be one for transgender men. There were interesting times ahead, and different sports would have to navigate these changes as best they could. He repeated the coaches' doctrine that the only constant is change.

Her blood began to boil, "But this is the *Women's* team," she said loudly, waving her arm in the direction of the training field. "*Women!*"

"That's only a name," he said. "I have to deal with reality."

ST. MONICA'S

AS CAPTAIN LEONARD LAY IN BED he contemplated the shape of a damp stain on the ceiling of his room in the nursing home, and wondered when his next humiliation was due. He didn't fully understand why Mark – the owner's son – had it in for him, and for other inmates. If he hated, or feared, old age so much why didn't he get a different job? Maybe he wasn't fit for anything else; the captain thought he may have heard something to that effect, but he couldn't be sure. His memory wasn't so good these days. He went back to the ceiling stain, which now looked like Australia – a continent he had a vague recollection of visiting when the world was young.

A timid knock on the door announced Katryn, a Polish girl who gave him his morning tea and a couple of biscuits.

"Two sugars, Captain?" she queried. "That is correct, yes?"

He nodded and might have managed a smile if he'd had his teeth in. "Thank God for Katryn," he thought. In a way she reminded him of his long-dead wife – something about the wisps of fair hair that graced the back of her neck. He was sorry for what Mark had done to her and regretted not being able to go to her defence at the time.

The tea hadn't tasted like tea for the last

twenty years, but that wasn't due to Katryn; it was due to old age. Even his taste buds were kaput. He only took two sips. But he had another reason for being so abstemious. He wished to postpone for as long as possible the complex logistics of going to the bathroom. Was he now the same person who had seen action on Omaha Beach? It was inconceivable. He wondered, not for the first time, why he hadn't died when he hit ninety – some three years ago. It seemed ridiculous to be lingering on when his body was closing down inch by inch, function by function. He often thought his mind was gone or going and had no way of proving it one way or the other. The fact that he worried about it gave him some reassurance.

He must have nodded off for a while because when he opened his eyes Mark was looming over him in his white uniform.

"Ah, Cap'n, my Cap'n, you're awake. Anything we can do for you?"

"No … thank you." Captain Leonard wished he'd go away and leave him alone.

"Do I detect a note of irritation? Let me guess. You've soiled yourself again? Am I right? Or maybe that's your normal whiff."

The old man kept quiet. If he rose to the bait he would pay for it in any number of ways. He just had to allow himself to be used as a punch bag and hope the younger man would tire of the game sooner rather than later. Several months ago he'd asked Mark to his face why he treated him so badly and the reply came: "Because I can." And it was true. There was no one to complain to and even if there were, it would only make matters worse. Mark had already taken advantage of Katryn with impunity. As a recent immigrant trying to get on her feet, she had no recourse whatsoever. During a long career, the captain had come across a few psychos in the army and was able to deal with them, or at least put a stop to the trouble they caused. But here in St. Monica's, at his advanced age, he was powerless.

"Why so quiet, Cap'n? I'm sure you had plenty of orders to bark at your servants in Wagga Wagga land. We've a new guy on the staff from Uganda. Maybe we'll get him to carry you around and wipe your backside. How would you like that? The white man's burden in reverse... Oh look, you didn't finish your tea." Mark picked up the cup and brought it towards the captain's lips.

"Cold ... too cold now..." The old man tried to avert his face as far as his rickety neck would allow.

"It's fine. We mustn't waste any of this nourishment." Mark crumbled a biscuit into the cup and forced fed it to the captain, who eventually submitted. "That wasn't so bad now was it? We should all be team players. That's what my teachers used to say. Did you know I went to military school to learn discipline? I'm one of their star pupils. We don't want any loose cannons on deck, Cap'n. Maybe that's why you don't have any visitors. Are you a loose cannon?"

"No…" The old man coughed and some of the biscuit crumbs adhered to his chin.

"Louder."

"No."

"Good. Now go back to sleep and dream about my next visit which will be very soon."

The captain had an uncomfortable night. He knew that Mark was abusive towards others, but he did seem to single him out for special treatment – apart from Katryn, of course, who had suffered most of all. It would get worse and worse because they were all powerless. They were all at the mercy of a bully who was himself probably a coward. There had to be a solution. What was it his C.O. used to say? There was always a solution if you were prepared to pay the price. He listened to the radio for a while – the one comfort he had left – and eventually drifted off to sleep when the predawn light began to seep through the muslin curtains on his window.

When Katryn brought him his morning tea at eleven he asked her to sit with him for a little while. She did so with a smile but seemed nervous, afraid that Mark might walk in on them. At his request she showed him how to operate her mobile phone – he had to use his magnifying glass to read the tiny keys. She agreed to leave the cell phone with him for an hour or so.

He wasn't sure exactly what he was trying to

achieve. It could be irrational or even insane for all he knew. There was no one to bounce ideas off, no touchstone. It was like the year he'd spent alone in a room after his wife died. The sense of unreality had become stronger and stronger until it enveloped him completely. In a way it had broken him; he never had the same confidence about any decision after that... He tried to put it out of his mind and, after repeated errors and false starts, he managed to manipulate the midget intricacies of the phone, and made the call to a former friend and colleague.

On Sunday afternoon he heard the appalling waltz music drifting along the corridors. The management brought in a keyboard player on Sunday afternoons to jolly the inmates along and impress the visitors, most of whom were paying through the nose for their coffin-dodging relatives. All of the inmates were expected to congregate in the foyer around the musician and waltz around in their carpet slippers. Captain Leonard dreaded it and his heart sank even further when he heard Mark working his way along his corridor, knocking on doors and barking at patients to assemble for the dance. The knocks came closer and closer, Gestapo knocks.

"Cap'n, my Cap'n, why aren't we out doing the light fandango? Or a Valetta at least. Remember what we discussed about team players?"

"I would like ... to be excused..."

"It's a command performance. Now, come on. Haul your skinny ass out of that chair." Mark took him by the arm but the captain resisted.

"I don't wish to…"

The feigned crooning altered suddenly. "What's this? Insubordination? Do what you're told, you old fart. I could break this arm like a twig." Mark increased his grip on the thin arm, no bigger than a turkey leg.

"I'll go."

"There's a good soldier. If you dance well I may even get you some Viagra and you can have any of the old crones you want. Not Katryn of course. She's mine." On the way out, Mark picked up the captain's radio and threw it on the ground. "Sorry, that was clumsy of me."

Captain Leonard shuffled around to the electronic dance music in his carpet slippers. Because of the amplification of the keyboard and the deafness of the dancers there was no possibility of conversation, and no one even made the effort to speak. Eventually, and to his great relief, his visitor arrived and linked him down the corridor to his room. They went in and closed the door behind them while the keyboard player enjoined the ghostly dancers to take their partners for the 'Blue Danube'.

Mark took a few days off in lieu of the weekend but early on Friday morning he called into the captain's room.

"So, who's the mystery man?"

"Who?"

"Your visitor. The codger who came to see you on Sunday afternoon. He got you off dance detail." Mark sat on the edge of the bed. "An illegitimate sprog?"

"A young army colleague…" Captain Leonard tried to keep the peace. There was a look in Mark's eyes he hadn't seen before; it frightened him.

"Young?"

"He was young … when we soldiered together."

"But he never bothered to visit you before. Why now?"

"Passing through…"

"Are you going to leave him something in your will?"

"Not your business." Captain Leonard turned his face on the pillow, and hoped that Mark would get bored and back off.

"What did you say?"

"You heard."

Mark loomed over him. "Say it again, you old fool."

"It's not your concern. It's my business."

Mark bent closer. "Listen, you wizened little fucker, with one hand I could press on your windpipe and snuff out your miserable existence. No one would know. Or care."

"Do it." The captain felt his heart move up a gear but he wasn't frightened anymore.

"I can do it slowly … very slowly … increasing the pressure a little at a time."

"Go ahead." The moment had come sooner than he wanted or expected but it had to happen some time.

"OK, you asked for it."

Just as Mark reached out his right hand Captain Leonard moved slightly to his left. The eiderdown shifted just enough to reveal a snubnosed revolver in his right hand. The barrel was pointing directly at Mark's chest.

"What…!"

"Don't move an inch."

"Put that down." Blood drained from Mark's face. Instinctively, he began to back away.

"I said don't move." Captain Leonard cocked the gun.

"You're not going to … probably not loaded… Look, just put it down."

"No. I want you to apologise to all of the clients. And to Katryn … and turn yourself in … to the police."

"Apologise…? What are you…? Well… maybe we could work something out…" As he spoke, Mark reached behind him towards the water jug on the bed-table. He knew the old man's sight was poor. He kept talking in a conciliatory way even as his groping fingers fastened around the heavy jug. He moved quickly. Just before he brought it crashing down on the captain's head a shot rang out. Mark's body jerked back as the bullet passed through his chest. He fell sideways on the bed.

With failing strength, the captain brought the

gun to his own temple. At the moment he was about to pull the trigger, he felt Mark's hand grip his throat. He changed aim and fired again. The bullet went through Mark's head, leaving a large exit wound. Again, the captain placed the muzzle against his temple and pulled the trigger several times but the chamber was empty. He had only asked for two bullets. He let the gun fall from his hand and fell back exhausted, just as the door flew open…

There was no doubt in Detective Daly's mind about what had happened. He had carried out exhaustive interviews and all the bits fitted together into a coherent whole. He wasn't entirely convinced that the old man had tried to kill himself but felt it was plausible. The victim had clearly been a mental case who couldn't hold down a normal job; indeed he was known to the police. His father had to shoulder much of the blame for employing him at St. Monica's. And for that he would be forced to sell the nursing home to a proper management team. Daly had encouraged Katryn to press charges and he felt that she might do so, now that she no longer went in fear of her employers.

The difficult question was whether to prosecute Captain Leonard or not. Dragging a frail ninety-three year-old war hero through the courts was problematic. The chances were he would kick the bucket half way through. Nevertheless, the State would probably feel obliged to prosecute, but what good would it do? It was a lose / lose proposition whatever way he sliced it. And if the old boy survived the court case were they really going to send him to prison?

Detective Daly reached a decision. With a little more than the usual bureaucratic red tape, he could delay the book of evidence for one or even two years. Then after that, the lawyers would take another year or two. Nature, in the meantime, would probably take its course.

The story did hit the newspapers and the Health Department was under the cosh for failing to inspect the nursing home properly. They lost no time in arranging a take-over. The new management of St Monica's was a family with a long and sound tradition in geriatric care.

One evening in late summer when migrating birds assembled on the walls of the garden, about to take their leave, Captain Leonard, on a Zimmer frame, shuffled into the dining-room. A ripple of applause made him look up. Katryn gave him a broad smile and escorted him to his table.

TAKE CARE

STILL CHEWING A MOUTHFUL of toast, Seb Platt brushed his wife's cheek with his, and took hold of his briefcase on the hall stand. Earlier, over breakfast, he had told her about his recent meeting with the CEO of his company. He was a little surprised to hear that his wife agreed completely with the advice his boss had given him. In fact, she reminded him about it on the doorstep, as he made to leave.

"Do you really think it's necessary?" he asked.

"Absolutely. Look, it's terribly important nowadays."

"I suppose..."

"Don't suppose. Just do what has to be done..." She waved until he reached the garden gate, then she went inside pulling the door after her. She heard the familiar sounds of the latch-bolt shooting into the lock and the knocker clunking back.

He walked down the avenue and turned left on to the main road; he was lucky with the buses and managed to read most of his newspaper on the top deck despite the constant ape chatter of mobile phone users.

He had just got off the phone with a client when one of his copywriters, Linda, knocked on the door of his office and walked in. He rose immediately and, in confusion, ushered her back out into the corridor.

"What is it...? she asked in surprise. "I thought you wanted to see the storyboards for..."?

"I do ... but ... something's changed..."

"What...? She seemed mystified.

He suggested that she go back to her desk; he promised to call her in a little while.

"Very strange," she murmured as she turned and walked back towards the elevators, winding the ends of her fair hair around a pencil.

She sat at her desk and went over the story boards one more time while waiting for his call. *Sepal Skin Products* was her first big account and she worked hard on getting the ad campaign to this level. She was hoping that Seb would sign off on it soon so that she could present the entire advertising plan to the board. She saw Seb, not as a hazard to navigation but as a mentor; she valued his input. He had been with the firm for much longer than she, and he had a good reputation for helping more junior people, both creatively and in relation to office protocols and politics. Almost all of his staff had done well in the company and that was largely down to him.

The way he had ushered her into the corridor wasn't like him. And he had seemed ... what exactly...? Uneasy ... yes, that was it. She laughed suddenly. Maybe he was rushing to the loo. That would definitely embarrass him. He was a rather sensitive soul, and though in his early forties had the manners of a much older man. Her friend, and neighbour in the open-plan space, brought her a coffee and plonked it down on her desk, taking care to avoid the artwork.

"Thanks, Liz." Linda smiled up at her. "My turn tomorrow."

"Oh, let's not keep count," Liz replied. "Hey, I thought you were going to see Seb in his office this morning to sign off on these terrific illustrations." She waved her ringed hand over the artwork as if casting a spell on it.

"I was. But for some reason he postponed the meeting. I'm waiting for him to call."

"Sounds odd. Still, stranger things happen at sea."

Just then a phone rang, but it wasn't Linda's. She looked around to see another colleague, Barney Steadman, pick up the receiver. She heard him say, "Yes, Mr. Platt, right away." As he got up from his desk she asked him where he was headed and he told her that Seb had asked him to drop into his office. He threaded his way through the open-plan area, avoiding plants and watercooler, and disappeared around the corridor.

"What's going on?" Liz asked.

"Damned if I know." Linda's puzzlement increased when her phone rang and Seb invited her to drop into his office.

"Will I come right away?" she asked, wishing to allow time for him to finish his meeting with Barney.

"Yes," he said, "as soon as you can."

The two women exchanged surprised glances. Liz went back to her desk, and Linda, again armed with her drawings, hastened along the corridor.

"Now, what've you got for me?" Seb inquired, showing her to a seat.

"Well…" She began, but faltered because she couldn't understand why Barney was sitting in the other visitor's chair. The *Sepal Skin Products* account had nothing to do with him. As if sensing her feeling of awkwardness, Seb told her he had asked Barney to sit in on the meeting. Then he quickly asked to see her work. She was keen to know why he had asked Barney to be present but she could hardly inquire straight out. His office, his rules. Besides, he hadn't volunteered an explanation and that must have been a deliberate choice. As she began to describe the concept behind the campaign she sensed that Barney was also ill-at-ease. It didn't seem as if he was making a play for the account; on the other hand there was also the possibility that he could be given the project if she didn't pass muster.

So her presentation did not go as smoothly as she would have hoped, and Seb was judging not just the content of the campaign but also her ability to make a presentation, since she would have to go before the board and quite possibly the client as well. All these thoughts unsettled her as she spoke. She explained as best she could how the important demographic was one which put 'youthful' skin above all else; hence the script that was to go with the visuals had to cover a little of the science of rejuvenation. That, she argued, should not be seen as boring but rather as a powerful means of persuasion.

Seb thanked her and opened the door for her and Barney. They both walked back to the open-plan area.

"Good job," Barney said.

"Thanks, but why were you there? You're not involved in this account."

"Don't ask me." He rolled his eyes towards the coffered neon of the ceiling. "Seb just asked me to sit in on your session. It never happened before, not to me, anyhow."

"He must have given some explanation?" She gave him a questioning glance.

"No, nothing. Nada. Maybe he just wants me to have additional experience. Christ, maybe he thinks I'm a dimwit."

"No." She thought it could be the beginning of a policy to turn in-house presentations into a kind of seminar. In a way it could make sense. However, she didn't like being a guinea-pig.

She discussed it with Liz in a bar after work, but she couldn't explain it either.

"Ask Seb," she suggested.

Linda mulled this over for a while and then made a slight grimace of distaste. "I can't really. It's up to him to volunteer the information. It was his decision."

"Maybe it will all become clear over the next few days. But," Linda put down her glass and held up a finger, "if I were you I'd watch my back. You're quite young to have an account like that. And there are plenty of older guys who would like to have a crack at it."

Liz thought she was being a little paranoid but held her peace. Both women gathered up their purses and headed for the railway station.

That evening, Seb told his wife that he'd done as she suggested. She seemed pleased and a little relieved. They stood together leaning over a countertop in the kitchen, chopping vegetables.

"I felt bad about it, though." Seb confessed, his eyes welling up from the onions. "It wasn't easy."

"At least you did it. That's the main thing." She raised her head to watch the news on the small kitchen TV. "The world has changed, Seb. Things that weren't even thought about yesterday are now essential. We have to adapt."

"That's more or less what the CEO said too."

"Well she's right.

He shook his head sadly, "I guess … but isn't it sad that it's come to this?" He went back to his chopping board.

Linda was no wiser and tried to put the matter out of her head while she worked on the *Sepal* account to bring the campaign to the next stage, which in office parlance was the '3D' stage, requiring real sets, models and camerawork. After lunch on Wednesday, Liz came and perched on her desk.

"I'm kind of busy…"

Liz put a finger to her lips and jerked her head in the direction of the Ladies. She made sure the stalls were unoccupied and then told Linda that she could now explain the mystery. Most of the male managers and departmental heads had decided to have a chaperone present in their offices when interfacing with women staff. As far as she could figure out Linda said that this development would not be announced officially by management or put in writing. She thought that it had the blessing of the CEO. Seb was merely the first to do it. But others had followed his lead.

"I don't believe it," Linda said. "Who on earth is going to shout, 'rape'? … I mean it's ludicrous."

"Apparently it has been triggered by the 'Me Too' movement and the allegations made about that judge, Kavanaugh."

"It's crazy! I mean who's going to believe that Seb made a pass…" She couldn't decide whether she wanted to laugh or cry.

"Who's going to believe he didn't? … unless there's a witness present." Liz shrugged as if to suggest that the new 'nonpolicy' could at least be rationalised.

Worse was to happen. Linda normally accompanied Seb to a seminar on Advertising Cinematography in Toronto in early autumn, but this time he decided to go on his own. She knew why, and when he returned she called him. Barney, who was in the office when she raised the matter, looked uncomfortable.

"I can't confirm or deny." Seb said. He felt miserable. Linda was the last person in the world to exploit any situation. But the CEO was definite: No exceptions. There would be no accusations of sexual assault on her watch. Seb had asked her to issue a policy statement that would explain her thinking to the staff, but she declined.

"What about my presentation to the Board?" Linda inquired.

"That will go ahead as planned."

"With or without a chaperone?"

He almost said that no chaperone would be needed since there would be several Directors present including the CEO. But that would be tantamount to admitting to the new 'nonpolicy'. So he just repeated that her presentation would go ahead as planned.

After a vigorous game of squash, the CEO invited Seb for lunch in the squash club. They went their separate ways to shower and then met up in the dining room. She, Veronica, was dressed in a formal business suit and had her hair scraped back in a bun.

"I almost had you there in the third set," she said to Seb. She preferred to play with men because they gave her a hard workout, and she was good enough to make it interesting for them.

"Your backhand could do with a little work."
He gave his order to the waiter.

"How is the new 'nonpolicy' working out?"
she asked when the salads arrived.

"It's awkward, Veronica, especially when
you're dealing with decent, trustworthy women. I
sense they feel the chaperone is a kind of insult."

"I get that. But what's the alternative?
Cameras in offices? I don't think so. The game-
changer for me was the Kavanaugh business...
Women deliberately trying to ruin the careers of
competent men. The third- and fourth-wave
feminists have gone too far. They've achieved
everything and still want more. I think the
pendulum is just about ready to swing back." She
signalled to the wine waiter and ordered two
glasses of Chablis.

"I wonder if the 'nonpolicy' isn't a
sledgehammer to crack a nut?"

"Yes and no. Most of the women in your
department are married and several have
children, right?"

"Yes. I often see the strain they're under. In
fact I think they're ageing faster than normal.
But it's what they want..."

"I wonder if it is? It could be propaganda.
Cultural Marxism. Career *and* home. I had to let
my secretary go because she spent a lot of time
going to the crèche when her kid was poorly, and
the rest of the time worrying about him. We're
not a charity, Seb. I made a conscious decision to
put career first. I postponed having children and

then when my marriage broke up I decided to forgo a home life. I'm not complaining. But young women nowadays think they can have it all. They think there are no trade-offs. And the radical feminists and SJW people reinforce that view. But it's patent nonsense."

"Well, it's certainly difficult for them," Seb put in. He sat back to allow the waiter place his fish course on the table. "But you said 'yes and no'?"

"I did. The chaperone idea isn't very efficient is it?" She broke off and told the waiter to bring a fish knife for Seb." It means that two people are now required where one used to be the norm. Also, it's come to my attention that women are requesting female chaperones... I think we should drop the chaperone."

"Oh OK, go back to where we were." It would be a relief to him.

"Absolutely not. The answer is staring us in the face. And now that the pendulum is set to swing back..."

"You don't mean...?" He held a napkin to his mouth to remove a fish bone as politely as he could.

"Yes. I'm afraid I do. There's no alternative. Male managers should delegate the important accounts, the ones that need hand-holding, to other men. We won't shout this from the rooftops, Seb, but in my opinion there's no other way. The fourth-wave feminists and the Professors of gender studies have turned women into liabilities rather than assets. They will have to be sidelined at least for the time being. Talk about unintended consequences! I don't think we should recruit women any more either. We have no way of filtering out the troublemakers. Anyway, we are liberal enough, taking on transgenders and gays, but ordinary women are now the problem."

Seb spent the rest of the meal arguing against this course of action but Veronica's mind was made up and he knew how stubborn she could be, and how she had the Board eating out of her hand. She repeated her belief that the zeitgeist was on the cusp of change and she wanted to be at the leading edge. Seb made a special case for Linda, so that at least, she could complete the project she was working on. Veronica was at first unmoved. Seb then explained how much work Linda had already put into the account and Veronica reluctantly agreed that she could carry it forward to final presentation.

Before going their separate ways in the car park, Veronica said, "Men are back in fashion, Seb. Oh and by the way, the Office Picnic and Christmas party are cancelled. Tell your staff."

After making her presentation, Linda was on a high. But she, Liz and the other women copywriters soon discover that the cards are stacked against them. They are not asked to handle the larger accounts and there are no explanations forthcoming. Barney is given an advertising campaign for table-linen products which Liz had banked on getting. She went to the Equality Agency, but when asked for evidence couldn't provide any. Linda sought other jobs but without success. For the first time in her life she thought that her gender told against her. She could hardly believe it. She derived no fulfilment from her work and was deprived of bonuses, so she resigned after a year and became a full-time homemaker. After a while she had to admit that it wasn't too bad, especially if routine could be avoided. But then with two young children there was never a dull moment. They saved a lot of money on crèches, baby-minding, commuting, take-outs, professional cleaning, and so on. She had to admit that her husband did his fair share in the home, even though he carried a lot of responsibility at work. She had a third child, a boy, while she was still in her thirties, and she liked being close to him.

A couple of years later she ran into Seb in a supermarket. His wife had died and he had taken early retirement after that. Linda had met him at his wife's funeral but didn't have an opportunity to talk to him then.

"I hope you're looking after yourself," she said. She knew how much he had depended on his wife.

"Doing my best… I was so sorry about all that business back then, Linda." He had a far-away look in his eyes

"I could sense that," she admitted. "I never thought your heart was in it."

"What killed me was the idea that you, of all people, might lay false charges against me or anybody else. It was a sledgehammer approach. We should have been more discriminating. You and many of the other young women suffered because of a small number of radicals. It was most unfair."

"The real problem was that no one could identify the troublemakers, the false accusers..."

"Yes. So the net was thrown wide."

"I always reckoned Veronica was behind it..."

He nodded. "She was most insistent... But she was right about one thing." He outlined Veronica's theory of the pendulum swinging too far. He didn't think it proper to say that his late wife was in full agreement.

"Interesting... And now of course the pendulum is swinging too far in the other direction."

"It seems so," Seb said. "It's a pity we can't find an equilibrium that everyone is happy with."

"Well, we adapt, don't we ... we humans ... we have to..." She couldn't help looking into his trolley to see if he was buying proper food. It wasn't too bad but there were some give-away ready meals for one. She thought of her own family and consulted her watch. "I must go. It was good to run into you."

"Take care, Linda."

"You too."

THE MUNSTER SWIMMER

MRS. WHELAN ROLLED ANOTHER floury potato on to her daughter's plate. Betty looked at it for a while and shook her head before reluctantly adding a wedge of butter.

"Are you on a diet or what?" her mother inquired.

Betty nodded. "The Coach brought in a diet expert. We have to watch the carbs."

Mrs. Whelan sniffed, not impressed at all by her family's food needs being outsourced to professionals. "It's supposed to be a sport."

"I know," Betty said. "But Coach Timlin is really keen for us to beat Presentation this year. He thinks I have a chance in the crawl and breaststroke."

"Don't make me laugh," her older brother said with a snort. "You swim like a rhinoceros. You're no Mark Spitz."

"Who's Mark Spitz?"

"Anyway, you need carbs for swimming. More blubber to keep you afloat. That's the only reason you can do the dog's paddle in the first place."

"Very funny." Betty tried to ignore her brother's jibe. But she did want to be a better swimmer. She wasn't as smart as her older sister and it would be some consolation if she had a few medals hanging from her belt. She didn't fancy her chances though; she just wasn't tall or strong enough and there was nothing she could do about it. It was all down to genes.

After the next training session Betty was just about to leave the locker room when Coach Timlin approached her. He was wearing a tracksuit and had a whistle on a lanyard around his neck.

"Well, Betty, how're you shaping up for the meet against Presentation?"

"Ah, not too bad, I suppose."

"That doesn't sound very confident," the Coach said.

"I'm just being realistic. My times aren't great. And I'm not … all that strong."

"It's all up here." The Coach tapped his noggin through the fabric of the baseball cap. "Look at the Munster rugby team. If they were the national squad they'd have won the World Cup. They have self-belief. That's what it's all about."

Betty kept her own counsel. She wasn't convinced. Maybe if she were taller, with a long back like Phelps had, or if she had those quick-twitch muscles … She had seen some of the Presentation girls with the broad shoulders and four- if not six-pack stomachs. They had the physiques of young men. "It's very competitive" she said.

"Follow me." The Coach led her out to the car park and stopped beside his metallic silver Toyota Avensis. He reached into the car and fetched a small cardboard box from the glove compartment. From the box he plucked a sachet of cellophane which contained about a dozen pink capsules.

"Take one of these every night," the Coach said.

Betty did a double take, "Wha-a-t?"

"It's all right," the Coach said. "It's not the Olympics and these aren't anabolic steroids. Just something we call *equalisers*. They'll help you get to the next level. No side effects, I swear. And they can't be detected. Go on, take them."

Betty hesitated and the Coach forced the packet into her hand. "One a night before bed. Trust me. It's not wrong. But don't tell anyone else, even your family. They wouldn't understand."

The next time Betty was in the pool she trained as hard as she could, following the routines the Coach had written on a blackboard near the deep end. She wasn't sure whether the pills had made any difference or not – there were no side-effects either – but she was bothered by the fact that she was on the way to becoming a cheat. Coach Timlin gave her some pointers about technique then asked with a knowing look whether things were going as planned.

"Yes," Betty said, half-hoping she would be told to forget about the pills.

"Good, stick with the plan," the Coach said, and that was all he said.

After the next training session, the Coach took her aside in the locker room and said,

"Do you want the good news or the good news?"

"There's no bad news?" Betty asked.

"No. It's all good." He held out a bunch of charts. "I've been looking at your times. You shaved one and a half seconds off the crawl and nearly one off the breaststroke. That's pretty good."

"That's fantastic." Betty could scarcely believe it, though while swimming she had a sense of better, smoother coordination, combined with a new, more relaxed rhythm. She also felt stronger and was able to breathe more easily.

"Now, remember," the Coach said in a barely audible voice, "just one tab at night. No more. OK?"

The next session was the last before the meet with Presentation. Betty swam well, continuing to improve, and was complimented by some of her teammates. Coach Timlin was pleased with her and he gave them all an upbeat team-talk. They had rarely beaten Presentation in the past but this time it was going to be different. This time they were going to win individual medals and the team cup. Their photographs would be put up in the school corridors to be admired by later generations of students.

During the talk Betty couldn't help wondering if the other girls were also on the tablets but she couldn't very well ask. And of course they couldn't ask her. It was a sort of silent conspiracy. But the important thing was that they wouldn't be competing against each other, not really. Anyway was it really cheating? It was possible that Presentation were on something too. Maybe they had been for years. If so it was about time they'd levelled the playing field – or pool in this case.

The Coach followed her out to the car park and gave her another two sachets.

"I want you to increase the dose to one and a half tabs a night between now and the competition."

"One and a half?"

"Yes. No more and no less. Here." He handed her a small cardboard box.

"What's this?"

"A pill-cutter. Use it so you can make exact halves."

"Should I not…?" Betty hesitated.

"What?"

"You know, go off them a couple of days before the competition?"

"No. There's no need. These are undetectable. Trust me."

On the morning of the competition, the team met at the school, got their gear ready and boarded a bus which brought them to a hotel where they had a light lunch. There was an air of excitement and much nervous chatter. Coach Timlin wasn't quite able to disguise his own nerves and this had the effect of making the swimmers even more edgy.

"It's no harm to be nervous," Coach Timlin

said several times. "It's good. Use the adrenalin. Put it to good use. Butterflies in the tummy will help you, especially if you're doing the butterfly stroke." His attempt at levity fell flat; this was not the time for laughter.

Hearts beat even faster when they arrived at the pool and could hear the chanting and singing of spectators from inside the echoing, high-ceilinged complex. When they were togged out and when they'd completed their stretching exercises Coach Timlin gave them a final team talk, in which the positive use of adrenalin was mentioned a few more times.

The first event was the breaststroke, and Betty almost recoiled from the wall of noise that greeted her as she walked out to the pool and took her place on the block. She adjusted her goggles, swim hat and the hem of her swimsuit. Two other teammates were also in this race as well as three from Presentation. Betty could hear her heart pounding as she waited for the starting pistol. She didn't get the best of starts. But when she surfaced she quickly established a rhythm – arms, legs and breathing, all working in synch. Her arm-pull was strong and it lifted her out of the water on each stroke. Every time her head came above the surface she heard the echoing cheers, some of which seemed to be for her. She gradually made up ground on the leaders and since she didn't feel out of breath this gave her confidence. In the last twenty-five metres she barely felt the lactic acid in her legs and even upped the stroke rate. She had a stitch in her side but swam through it. To her surprise she won the event. As she dragged herself out of the pool, she knew that most of the cheering was directed to her. She gave a shy wave in response.

She got a better start in the front crawl, developed an early lead and hung onto it. The water seemed to offer less resistance than she could ever remember. At times she felt as if she were hydroplaning. Her breathing was smooth and rhythmic. She actually enjoyed being in the pool competing in a race. It had never felt like that before. She won the crawl though not by very much. But she had won it. And with two first prizes in the bag she would be awarded two medals and of course she had contributed a considerable number of points to the team score.

She was pummelled and congratulated in the locker room, and the Coach was ecstatic with the first school victory over Presentation in twenty years. As they were walking out to board the bus a dark-suited man was seen talking to the Coach, who called Betty back into the locker room. The other man, a doctor, asked Betty for a urine sample. The process was civilised and efficient; no one spoke. When Betty got back on the bus the euphoria had subsided and she was conscious of strange looks from her teammates.

"Why me?" Betty asked the Coach afterwards. Her heart was still in her shoes.

"I suppose it's your rate of improvement, Betty. Your speed developed very quickly. The

Presentation Coach probably suspected something. But don't worry about it."

Betty did worry. She'd never been lionised before and she liked how it felt. She certainly didn't want to give back the medals or be humiliated. She had sleepless nights and her mother was confused by her attitude. At first her mother put it down to a sense of anticlimax after the great success, but then she began to worry when her mood didn't lift. To make matters worse she just couldn't get a word out of her. For her part, Betty began to fantasise; if it really got ugly she could blame the Coach. No, she couldn't do that. OK, Timlin gave her the pills but he didn't force them down her throat. She would have to take responsibility.

When, eventually, the results came back from the lab Betty kept the unopened envelope in her pocket until lunchtime. She waited in the schoolyard until Coach Timlin joined her. Then she opened the letter and read quickly.

She raised her head. "Negative...," she read uncertainly. "Negative," she repeated more firmly. "That means clear. I'm clear! I'm clear!" She punched the air. She would have the respect of her pals again.

"I told you not to worry," Coach Timlin said, smiling.

"How could you be so sure?"

"Sugar."

"What?"

"The pills contained sugar and food

colouring, nothing else."

"What…? Why?" Betty was shaken.

"I had to let you prove to yourself how good you really are. It's all in the mind, Betty."

"But I was worried stiff…"

"I'm sorry about that. But at least you'll remember."

"I'll remember all right." Betty knew she'd been manipulated, but she also felt the mood of elation drifting back. And the feeling of guilt was gone. She had done it all by herself, unaided.

"Do you believe in yourself now?" The Coach asked.

"Well, I suppose…"

"My God, you're prevaricating again. How much proof do you need? I'm going to ask you again. Do you believe in yourself now?"

"Yes."

"I can't hear you."

"Yes!" Betty shouted. Startled rooks flew out of nearby trees.

AN ACCOUNTING

TREASSA CLERY'S NORMALLY RELAXED FACE wore a tight and worried expression. Her friend, Bernadette, who had been throwing her questioning glances from her workstation, finally jerked her head to one side, indicating that she wanted to have a chat. They converged on the photocopier – the office didn't have a water-cooler. Bernadette knew there was something wrong but the younger woman seemed strangely reluctant to discuss it, which made her friend all the more eager to find out what was bothering her. After much hesitation and false starts, Treassa finally got it off her chest.

"I think … I may have been … harassed…" Even as the words came out she seemed surprised by them, even a little embarrassed.

Bernadette tried to calm her down and told her to start at the beginning. Treassa did so in a halting way, depending on her friend to give frequent nods of affirmation. It appeared that one of the Executives of the firm, Jack McKinnon, had called her into his office to discuss an audit she was working on. They sat at his round meeting table and went over the paperwork. He was nasty and nitpicking about her work and was generally in a foul mood.

"Did he bully you at any stage?" Bernadette inquired.

"I don't think so." Treassa had felt bullied

but it was the first time and she had learned from her induction course that bullying was defined as a continuing offence. If he harangued her *again* then she would have a case.

Bernadette confirmed that this was so. She was an expert in the new Equality Legislation and was working on a major case to bring the firm to court on behalf of all women employees. Despite equality of ability and qualifications there was not one woman Partner and only one had broken through the glass ceiling to become an Executive, and she had turned down marriage and family in the interest of her career.

Treassa continued with her account – they had moved into the corridor by now because one of the secretaries had come to use the photocopier. At the end of her fraught encounter with Jack McKinnon he had looked directly at her and, as if he were offering her an excuse for her poor work, asked if she was having a problem with her period.

"My God." Bernadette's face took on a very serious expression.

"What do you … think? I suppose it was a … form of …"

"Harassment? Of course it was… That creep… What exactly did he say? Exactly?"

"He'd been criticising my work as I said, and then at the end he wanted to know if I was having a problem menstruating."

"He actually used that word?"

"Yes."

"He's going to pay for that." Bernadette brought Treassa to her office where she dug out the relevant form. They helped each other filling it out. In the first part of the form a statement of the complaint had to be set out in detail; this was followed by a formal demand for an apology and for his promise never to offend again. They put it in a sealed envelope addressed to Jack McKinnon and stamped the envelope 'Personal and Confidential'.

"I suppose it is the right thing to do…" Treassa was a little nervous, taking on her boss like that, and needed the reassurance of the other woman who hugged her and patted her on the back.

"Of course it's the right thing to do. And between ourselves, this isn't the first time McKinnon has offended. He's due in the Tribunal any day now on another charge." The girls in the typing pool had a name for him: Premature Jack.

Treassa chewed her lower lip. What if her case, coming on top of the other one, landed McKinnon in real trouble? She really didn't want to make a Federal case out of it. Supposing it recoiled on her in some way. She voiced her concern.

Bernadette shook her head firmly. "It's time Neanderthals like him learnt how to behave in the workplace. It's not safe for any woman to get in the lift with him. It's time to call a halt. Your complaint and this other case, involving Daphne, should sort him out for once and for all. He's a groper, for God's sake."

"He didn't touch … I mean there was nothing like that …"

"He only touches…" Bernadette began but changed tack. "That's not the point. What you experienced was verbal and psychological abuse in a power relationship." She went on to explain how that could be even more damaging since it could undermine a person's confidence and self-esteem. No, Treassa had done the right thing and shouldn't think twice about it. Instead she should take the rest of the day off, hit the shops or the hairdressers.

"But the audit I'm working on is urgent." They parted briefly as the office boy rudely pushed his trolley between them.

"That's his problem." Bernadette emitted a brief snort. "Go on, get your hair done."

The following day Treassa received a memo from Jack McKinnon. It stated that he was surprised and dismayed by her accusation which was pure fabrication, perhaps the product of a feverish mind. There was no question of an apology, unless she wished to apologise to him. However, he would not insist on that since he realised that she was a little out of her depth in her work and therefore under stress.

Treassa read it several times and each time found it more chilling. The cold formality scared her, as did the forcefulness of the denial, which implied that she might be delusional. The patronising tone at the end was the least of her worries. She began to doubt herself; maybe she had misheard. She should have let it go and not allowed herself to be pushed around by Bernadette.

On seeing the memo, Bernadette was outraged. "Now you see what we're dealing with, a callous bastard and a liar. Can you imagine the arrogance of that person? Just because he's gotten away with it over the years. Who the hell does he think he's dealing with?" She rummaged through a drawer, scattering documents in all directions, until she found the form for the next, quasi-judicial stage. She made a few phone calls and got the case moved up the list. Before the afternoon was over she had a hearing date. The Tribunal would be chaired by Ms Riordan, an Equality Arbitrator, formerly a senior official in the Department of Justice. Bernadette seemed pleased both by the early date and the chairperson. She spent some time again reassuring Treassa that she had done the right thing. "We have to follow through," she insisted, "if he's to get the message. And, remember, there's no way you can lose. It's open and shut."

"But isn't it my word against his?"

"Ms Riordan will believe you. She knows that women don't make complaints without good reason. In fact they tend to be too reluctant to come forward. Don't worry about it."

"But I don't want to get Mr. McKinnon into real trouble either."

Bernadette raised a finger. "That's not your problem. He's a big boy. He has to be responsible for his own words ... and deeds." Just how arrogant was he, she wondered, thinking he could bluff his way out of this. She hoped he would be sacked and thought it quite possible since two of the senior partners were scrupulously correct politically and believed that the firm should have an unsullied reputation.

During the next few days both women spent a lot of time closeted together, going over the evidence such as it was, and discussing the protocols of the Tribunal. Bernadette also had separate sessions with the other woman, Daphne, who had been groped by McKinnon in the elevator.

On the due date the two complainants, accompanied by Bernadette who fussed over them, arrived early and waited outside the Tribunal chamber. They saw Jack McKinnon come in with his advisers. He didn't acknowledge their presence but gave them a look of disdain, though for a couple of seconds his glance lingered on Daphne who was, by any standard, eye-catching. Bernadette felt her skin crawl.

When the case was called, an usher brought them into the chamber where Ms. Riordan was presiding, and showed them to their places. Opening statements for the petitioners were made in relation to both charges. Ms Riordan was reading her papers, but it was clear that she was listening as well. When the depositions were tabled she turned to Jack McKinnon and asked him what he had to say about the first charge of groping.

Jack stood up, looking formal and well-groomed in his lightweight Italian suit, and said that he had never voluntarily touched a woman who didn't want to be touched.

"Are you saying," Ms Riordan inquired coldly, "that the petitioner wanted to be touched?" She removed her glasses, waiting for his reply.

"Not at all," he began. Nor did he deny that touching had occurred, but he insisted that it was an accident, completely beyond his control. Bernadette and Daphne exchanged glances and almost smiled; if this was the best he could do he was dead in the water. And, of course, Treassa's complaint would be upheld.

Ms Riordan looked perplexed and asked him to explain how touching could take place without his volition, how on earth it could be described as an accident.

Moving slightly to his left to avoid a shaft of dusty light from one of the Gothic windows, Jack McKinnon cleared his throat and said that sometimes his hand moved in involuntary spasms. No one in the room even tried to stifle their laughter.

Ms Riordan stared at him. "Try again, Mr. McKinnon."

"It's true, Madam Arbitrator," McKinnon

answered. "I suffer from these uncontrollable spasms. It's a medical condition…"

"A medical condition?"

"Yes. Mandelbaum's Syndrome. It manifests itself in different ways. In my case it's quite embarrassing. My left hand sometimes moves as if it had a life of its own."

Ms Riordan leant forward, resting her chin on a bridge of interlocked fingers. Bernadette rolled her eyes in incredulity for the Arbitrator's benefit. The silence was ripening nicely for the plaintiffs' cause when suddenly McKinnon's left arm flew out from his side and reached a forty-five-degree angle before dropping back. This time the laughter was sporadic and partially stifled.

Jack McKinnon launched into a fuller explanation. Specialists in Mandelbaum's Syndrome described his left hand as an 'anarchic limb' which could move suddenly in any direction. Indeed more than once it shot up and tried to choke him.

"An anarchic limb…?" Ms Riordan bit her underlip, which had begun to tremble. When she recovered her composure she asked if this was the sort of problem displayed by Peter Sellers in 'Dr. Strangelove'.

"The Nazi salute? Yes, Ma'am, exactly, although that was a melodramatic form. For artistic purposes, no doubt."

Ms Riordan asked if this was a recognised medical condition and if he had any certification of same by a doctor. McKinnon handed some documents to the usher who laid them on the bench. Ms Riordan examined them carefully, pushed them slightly to one side and looked up.

"There seems to be … something in what Mr McKinnon says. Mitigating circumstances at least…" The effort to be impartial told in her expression.

"Oh, my God…" Bernadette glanced in some distress towards each of her charges in turn. She hardly heard Ms. Riordan say that though this was a bizarre medical condition she could not ignore a doctor's report. The first charge was dismissed. But the second one of verbal abuse, directed at Ms Treassa Clery, could not be attributed to an anarchic hand. She had read the papers carefully and was at a loss to understand why Mr McKinnon did not apologise for his outburst. He didn't seem to have heard, so she put the question loudly to him.

"Why, Mr McKinnon, did you not apologise to Ms Treassa Clery for that dreadful and abusive reference to her monthly cycle?"

He looked steadily at her. "I had nothing to apologise for."

Ms Riordan pointed out in forceful terms that she was empowered to reach a conclusion on the balance of probability even where there was no hard evidence. She was tending towards a conclusion which would not be in his favour, but she would give him one last chance to apologise. If he did not do so she would press for maximum sanctions.

"Well?"

"Well what?"

"Are you going to apologise?"

"Absolutely not. There's nothing to apologise for." He went on to say that Ms Clery had been completely wrong in her allegation and that he was fed up with oversensitive, emotional women who preferred to entrap men instead of getting on with the job they were paid to do. If women genuinely wanted equality with men in the workplace they should start by behaving like adults instead of spoiled, manipulative brats. This outburst was greeted by a stunned silence. There was a mineral glitter in Ms Riordan's eyes. The anarchic hand may have been funny, albeit in a dark way, but this was not funny at all. It was downright sinister. She interrupted him and said sharply, "You give me no choice but to…"

"Before you embarrass yourself further," McKinnon cut in, "let me play you a tape. I record most of my 'gender' conversations as a form of protection." Before she had time to say anything he pressed the play button on a handheld recorder. In the silence of the chamber his and Treassa's voices could be clearly heard. He was questioning her about the audit she'd been working on and she was responding in a defensive, almost surly way. At one point she admitted to having made a mistake in depreciating property assets. Then he was heard asking her if she had a problem with menstruation.

"You *did* say it," Ms Riordan interrupted sharply.

"No, I did not. Listen to it again." He turned up the volume. This time Ms Riordan was deflated and clearly annoyed. The offending word was 'mensuration'.

"Do you get it now? I asked her if she had a problem with mensuration. If she has, I don't think she'll be a successful accountant or auditor. We have to uphold professional standards."

Ms Riordan's face was a mask. She looked coldly at McKinnon, then at the plaintiffs, and abruptly dismissed both charges.

Outside, Bernadette and the two plaintiffs were in a huddle of mutual disappointment. Jack McKinnon passed them by.

"Hard luck, Ladies. Be more careful next time. And remember, it pays to improve your word power." He waved as he walked down the steps, leaving one manicured finger aloft longer than the others.

"The bastard," Bernadette grated. "We'll get him one day, never fear."

The other two women sobbed quietly into their handkerchiefs.

"I just … want to go … home." Treassa said.

TOUCHING ON CONSCIENCE

WHEN EMMA FELL INTO the bunk bed at five in the morning she virtually passed out; it was more coma than sleep. Some fifty minutes later a long sharp needle skewered itself slowly through her exhausted brain. It was the vicious, relentless sound of her bleeper. With considerable effort she struggled upright into a sitting position, trying to focus her bloodshot eyes.

"Cardiac arrest... Ward 15... Cardiac arrest...!"

Emma managed to get out of the cot, shuddering as her feet hit the cold floor of the Interns' Room. She slipped on her shoes and started to run towards Ward 15. It had to be Mrs Hempenstall, even though she seemed stable the night before, no, earlier that same night. Still disoriented, Emma ran, not yet fully sure of the direction of Ward 15, but running nevertheless. As she ran she tried to muster another degree of consciousness.

"Emma!"

Was it her imagination or did someone call her name? She drew tangled strands of hair back from her eyes and saw her senior Consultant, Mr McGlancy, gesturing towards her. She intuited that he wanted to see her in his consulting rooms.

"But ... the emergency..." she blurted out.

"Who?"

"Ward 15... Probably Mrs Hempenstall."

"False alarm," he said, or at least that was what she thought he said. He pointed to the leather examining couch, bade her sit and indicated that he wanted a word with her.

Not yet fully awake, she again mentioned the bleeper, adding her fear that Mrs Hempenstall may have had a cardiac incident, possibly an infarction.

"False alarm," he said. She definitely heard him this time. "Sit. Relax." He loomed over her for a while and then lowered himself into an executive swivel chair which was specially contoured for his weak back. He was a tall man and for all of his trying years as a trainee surgeon he had to deal with operating tables that were set too low for him. Hence, the spinal stenosis. It wasn't until he became a senior Consultant that he was able to set the operating table to the height that best suited him, but at that stage his spine had already been damaged. "I take it you never got the lecture about how to answer an emergency bleeper?"

"No-o-o..." She had never seen him smile before; it was a little unsettling since he was normally so grim and bossy. What did he want? Had she screwed up yet again? He would certainly be capable of lulling her into a false sense of security and then dropping the boom on her.

He told her about the lecture, according to which the young hospital doctor should do everything in their power to avoid getting to the scene first, since that could land them in a world of pain and recrimination. The recommended course of action, on hearing the bleeper, was to sit down, read the front page of the newspaper and then, some five minutes later, run like hell and make sure to be seen running. "Rather cynical, don't you think?" He seemed interested in her answer.

"I'm sure it's not meant to be taken seriously." She felt a little silly sitting on the leather examining couch with her legs swinging.

"No, of course not. But there are always a few who take it to heart. Some of them go on to be very successful. Now, Emma, remind me, you've been a resident for how long?"

"Almost two years." Why was McGlancy in his rooms at such an early hour and what on earth did he want?

With one quick and sweeping glance he took her all in from stem to stern. She reminded him of himself at that age; an eager whippet answering every call, running around exhausted, taking things on with little regard for how they might work out. She was obviously working seventy-hour weeks, doing without a social life, agonising over the few mistakes she made. She probably didn't resent the seven tough years at college, the appalling pressure of hospital life, being hated by nurses, threatened with litigation by patients and their relatives, exploited by consultants, himself included.

"So, you hope to make Registrar in what …

another three years?"

"All going well." She smiled and gave a small shrug which indicated self-deprecation rather than indifference.

He noticed her sturdy white teeth and those frank blue eyes that had often caught his attention during Rounds. She was always eager to answer his questions, to volunteer for every task – often doing nurse's work when they were having their frequent breaks as far away from patients as they could manage to get. This young woman, despite her skill and zeal, would not make Consultant until her late thirties – if she were lucky. After years of neglect by civil servants and politicians, the system was toxic. It was not that they were short of beds, equipment or buildings. No, it was the frontline people who were diseased by the system. The best people left the hospitals to work for pharmaceutical companies and have some kind of life. Only the fools and the zealots stayed on. When they finally made Consultant they had a fifteen-year window for payback. Only then could they take revenge on the system that had completely drained them of motivation, initiative and any idealism they might have started out with. Only then could they take up golf, enjoy the hospitality of drug companies, take on wealthy private patients. He had done all three.

How many patients had died on his watch when he was a young intern, too exhausted to tell one form of medication from another and, how many had died later, when he was trying to make up for the life he had sacrificed until he was forty years old? How many? Too many.

Country people were right in their belief that one should stay out of hospital at all costs. It used to be a superstition, of course, but now it was fact. A hospital was like a 'Roach Motel' as advertised on American TV – a place where "the roaches check in but do not check out." Yes, the toxin had come full circle. The healing profession was now killing patients – and being well paid for it.

"You still have a vocation?"

"I ... hope so..." What was this avuncular stuff? Why was McGlancy, aka, *The Rottweiler*, being nice to her? No one would believe it.

"I suppose you used to bring home birds with broken wings and fix them up."

"Well, there was a frog once..." He must be losing it, she thought. He was well known as a stickler and prima donna, and she had heard one or two stories of how he had groped the more attractive nurses. People respected him as a Cardiologist, but they didn't really like him. Why was he being nice to her? She thought fondly of her bunk bed. Having been on the go for forty straight hours, not counting the fifty minute nap, she could do with another couple of hours in the sack instead of chewing the fat with McGlancy. Since the emergency had been a false alarm she really should be trying to catch up on some sleep. It was one thing to recharge her batteries but what if her batteries were so run down they couldn't hold a charge? Many of her colleagues had simply run out of energy.

"A what?"

"A frog. His legs were cut off by a lawnmower."

"Oh, I see ... I know I've been hard on you from time to time, but you didn't wilt. I remember that time in the OR when I let you touch a beating heart. There was such awe in your eyes..."

"I remember ... I thought I was touching the soul and conscience of the patient... It was one of those moments ... you never forget..." She was surprised that he recalled the incident.

"Anyway, with your level of commitment ... well, I think you'll make it."

"Thank you." A compliment from McGlancy. Wonders would never cease. This uncharacteristic behaviour made her even more confused. She watched as he phoned Catering and ordered breakfast for both of them. She really would prefer another couple of hours sleep but she could hardly turn down a breakfast ordered by him even if he hadn't consulted her about it.

"I never had a daughter," he went on, "So I had no terms of reference. I treated you exactly the same as the male residents."

"I wouldn't have wanted special treatment." He bullied them all equally; if he had been easier on her she'd have lost the respect of her peers.

She did wonder why *everyone* was treated so badly – zero tolerance and zero respect – and the only answer she could come up with was that it had been ever thus. That was the system. Was it possible that McGlancy was trying to apologise for his part in it; was it some sort of belated repentance? But why choose *her* ear to bleed into?

"Good." McGlancy recalled his own mentor, old Fogarty, long since gone to his eternal reward. What a bastard he was. He once asked McGlancy to scrub in long before he was ready, and made him suture an aorta on his own. Because of nerves and sheer lack of experience, he had accidentally raised an intimal flap on a coronary artery. Fogarty hadn't seen it either. Twenty-four hours later the artery thrombosed and the patient died from myocardial infarction. Fogarty would have had him fired if it weren't for the fact that he would have had to share some of the blame. He never let him forget it and he prevented McGlancy from becoming a Consultant until the day he retired. If McGlancy had come from a medical family it would have been very different, but he didn't have powerful forebears and was a perfect scapegoat for Fogarty. At least he learnt what 'Primum Non Nocere' really meant; it meant do no harm to yourself and cover your arse at all times. But even that practical maxim could not save a marriage.

"Try to have a life." McGlancy was surprised

to hear his own voice utter those words. He was hardly a good role-model, especially as his wife had walked out on him five months previously. No life, she'd said. The change of life, he'd countered. That was the trigger. No doubt, pressures and feelings of resentment had been building for months, maybe even years. But it escalated very quickly after that exchange; everything he said reinforced her view; everything she said was an insult to a man in his position. He felt cheated. How could she walk out on someone who devoted himself to saving life? What did that say about her core values? She called him a cardiologist without a heart.

"Medicine is a large part of my life," Emma said. Breakfast arrived. She sipped the coffee, hoping it might be decaffeinated; she still had designs on some more sleep. It was a savage urge; the thought of closing her eyes was sensual, overpowering, more compelling than a starving animal's desire for food. Even one hour would make a difference; it would get her through the day that was already bearing down on her.

"Don't let it interfere with ... relationships..."

"I'll try ... not to." For the first time she saw a pillow stuffed behind the sofa in his office. Had he been sleeping in his rooms? That would explain why he was in the hospital so early. She had heard something about his marital difficulties.

"You know, Emma, during Rounds I always picked you out of the crowd" He was smiling at her; a gold filling glistened. "You were always ready with answers ... good answers..." His voice tailed away. He ate a piece of croissant, then dabbed his mouth with a napkin.

"I learnt a lot..." What was the agenda? She began to feel uncomfortable.

"I always felt there was a..." He made a sawing action with his hands and then brought them together with a slight clap. "...a connection between us..."

"Professional, of course..." Oh God, she thought, don't let this happen. Please nip it in the bud. She hated his wrinkled, cyanosed hands.

"No, more than that, Emma. Even your name..." He reached out and stroked her hair with the back of his fingers. "And those blue eyes..."

"I must have given ... the wrong..." She slid off the examining table, pushed the breakfast tray away, looked at her watch. "God, that time already ... I have to..."

Suddenly his hand covered one of hers. His face was close to her face. She was aware of blurred red lips, grey stubble, stale aftershave. "Emma ... I always ... I need ... you must understand..."

She wriggled free of his clutching hands but he refused to get the message and followed up with renewed intensity. She was afraid for herself but also for him. How could smart men be such fools? Later, when he realised what he'd done he'd be absolutely mortified. Her resistance became stronger. "I'm sorry… Please stop… No, Mr. McGlancy!" Maybe it was the sound of his name that caused him to slacken his grip. In that split second Emma made a successful break. As she rushed through the door she heard his parting shot which, though delivered in relative calm, had a nasty sting in the tail.

"Don't do this to your career."

Relieved to be outside, her breathing was still laboured and his last comment resounded in her head. She walked the length of one corridor, then back again. Sleep was out of the question now, that precious hour completely gone. Consultants were gods; they had thunderbolts in their hands and used them often. Some had been abused early on; they repeated the pattern. She had just made a powerful enemy, a man who sat near the pinnacle of Mount Olympus. If she complained that he made a pass at her she'd be laughed at.

She was going back towards the Interns' Room but on an impulse went instead to Ward 15. She stood aside to allow a gurney past, then a crash cart. Outside the Ward she found a young intern in distress. She knew him vaguely from the recent intake.

"Why didn't you come?" His voice was on the point of breaking.

"I don't understand…"

"Mrs. Hempenstall died. Why didn't you answer? I couldn't cope on my own… Did you sit down and read ... the first page of the newspaper?" He began to sob. It was the first time he'd lost a patient.

"No, I..." There was nothing she could say. She leant against the wall; it wasn't that McGlancy had become unhinged, it was just that he had never tried to improve the system but allowed himself to be absorbed completely by it. She put her hand on the intern's shoulder and kept telling him that it wasn't his fault. In time he would come to believe that, and he too would lose his conscience.